CLAY

Also by Cheyenne McCray

Romantic Suspense

Zack: Armed and Dangerous
Luke: Armed and Dangerous
Kade: Armed and Dangerous
Moving Target
Chosen Prey

Suspense

The First Sin
The Second Betrayal

Urban Fantasy

Demons Not Included
No Werewolves Allowed
Vampires Not Invited

Paranormal Romance

Dark Magic
Shadow Magic
Wicked Magic
Seduced by Magic
Forbidden Magic

Erotica (writing as C. McCray)

Total Surrender

Anthologies

Real Men Last All Night
No Rest for the Witches

CLAY

Armed and Dangerous

Cheyenne McCray

ST. MARTIN'S GRIFFIN ☒

NEW YORK

CLAY: ARMED AND DANGEROUS. Copyright © 2011 by Cheyenne McCray. All rights reserved. Printed in the United States of America. For information, address St. Martin's Press, 175 Fifth Avenue, New York, N.Y. 10010.

www.stmartins.com

Library of Congress Cataloging-in-Publication Data

McCray, Cheyenne.
    Clay : armed and dangerous / Cheyenne McCray. — 1st ed.
        p. cm.
    ISBN 978-0-312-38670-2
    1. Women ranchers—Fiction.   2. Sheriffs—Fiction.   I. Title.
    PS3613.C38634c53 2011
    813'.6—dc22

                                                2010043560

First Edition: April 2011

10 9 8 7 6 5 4 3 2 1

To Gisele and Bird-Butt.
Thanks for keeping Spirit in line.

Author's Note

Clay: Armed and Dangerous has its basis in a story I wrote several years ago for an at the time small e-publisher.

Clay is easily the most erotic of the *Armed and Dangerous* series. Rylie Thorn and lawman Clay Wayland take their passion beyond the limits.

Rylie was a fun free spirit to write about and Clay a hunk in Western jeans. I hope you enjoy reading their story as much as I enjoyed writing it.

CLAY

Chapter 1

Rylie Thorn pulled at her earlobe as she guided her battered ranch pickup into the parking lot of the Cochise County Sheriff's Department. The stupid wreck bucked and hiccupped like it wanted to die, then steam billowed out from under its hood as she slammed on its bad brakes and threw it into park. The poor old work vehicle wasn't meant for driving distances, but it wasn't like she had a whole lot of choices.

None, in fact.

Rylie wished she could spit smoke like the wreck. Just driving the piece of shit was an unwelcome flashback to childhood. They had struggled so much. And her mom, the doormat . . . She shook her head.

Then and now. Big difference. Life wasn't easy, but it was nothing like her early years. Rylie knew things would get better soon, and she'd damned sure never be anybody's doormat.

She used an old rag in the seat to wipe sweat off her forehead. Air-conditioning? Of course, the beat-up hunk of junk didn't have any air. She jerked the keys out of the wreck's ignition and slammed the door as she got out. She'd had it up to *here* with the damn truck thefts, and she was determined to give the new hotshot sheriff a piece of her mind.

Rylie had been pissed about Skylar MacKenna's cattle being stolen last year, and now trucks were going missing all along the border. The Thorn Ranch had been ripped off. Things had definitely gotten *personal*.

She marched across the parking lot to the sheriff's office, her boot heels clattering against the pavement and her jeans skirt bouncing against the back of her knees. She had on short sleeves, and it was past hot already. Spring never could hold off summer in Douglas. Even though it was only April, the second the night's chill burned away in the morning, she started to sweat. Being furious didn't help that situation one bit.

She shoved the glass doors open and stomped into the reception area.

A busty brunette raised a sculpted eyebrow, her scarlet lips set in a what-the-hell-do-you-want smile. "May I help you?"

"I'd like to see Sheriff Wayland." Rylie propped her hands on her slim jean-clad hips. *"Now."*

"I don't think he's available." Boob Queen gave a don't-you-wish-he-was-available sniff as she picked up the phone. "Let me check."

Her temper escalating beyond eruption level, Rylie glanced past the reception area. She looked into a room that was empty save for desks sporting computers and equipment . . . and that sorry excuse for a deputy, Hazard Quinn. Young, dark-haired, too good-looking for his own good—Quinn was more country-music-star-to-be than skilled law enforcement—at least in his own mind.

Without so much as a by-your-leave, Rylie headed straight for Quinn. She set her gaze on stun with shoot-to-kill as an alternative if the deputy didn't give her satisfaction.

"You can't—" Miss Mega-Tits spouted behind Rylie.

"I need a word with you." Rylie strode right up to Quinn, propped her hands on her hips, and frowned up at him. At just five feet four, she only came to the deputy's shoulder—but her glare was enough to cut down a man three times her size. And Rylie knew how to wield her icy gaze like a sword.

Quinn's Adam's apple bobbed and he diverted his eyes, waving off Boob Queen, then turning his attention back to Rylie. "What do you need, Ms. Thorn?"

"I'll *tell* you what I need." Rylie poked one finger at his deputy's star, punctuating each word with a jab at the metal. "I need my trucks back. I lost five last night. *Five.* At the same time! Four of the ranch hands' vehicles, and my personal truck, too. I need you guys to get off your asses and figure out who the hell is stealing everybody's rides."

Quinn stepped back. "We're working on it. It's a borderwide problem."

"Don't give me that crap." Rylie advanced on the deputy as he retreated. "Get me the sheriff. *Now.*"

"What can I do for you?" A deep rumbling voice startled Rylie out of her tirade and sent shivers down her spine.

She whipped her head to the side and her gaze locked with the most amazing crystalline green eyes—and the hottest man she'd ever seen. Her entire body shivered, every coherent thought fleeing her mind as she got lost in the pull of those magnetic eyes.

He had his hip and shoulder propped against the doorway of an office, his thumbs hooked in the pockets of his snug Wrangler jeans, and a copper sheriff's star on his shirt. The man raised one hand to push up the brim of his tan felt Stetson as he studied her. His sable mustache twitched as he smiled.

Oh. My. God. For the first time in her life, Rylie Thorn was speechless.

Sheriff Clay Wayland studied the little wildcat who'd stormed into his office and ripped Deputy Quinn a new one. Damn she'd been cute as she'd spouted off at Quinn. Clay had enjoyed watching the flush in her fair cheeks, how her short blond hair shimmered as she spoke, and the way that sprinkling of freckles made her look so damn adorable.

He'd almost hated to interrupt her. And now . . . *well, hell.* The desire that sparked in those chocolate-brown eyes charged up his own libido. Something in his gut told him this was a woman worth getting to know—in every way a man could know a woman.

He pushed away from the door of his office and strode toward her. "Clay Wayland," he said as he held out his hand.

Quinn mumbled something about "work to be done," and headed on out of the office, leaving Clay alone with the woman in the empty control room.

"Rylie Thorn." The petite woman drew herself up and raised her chin as she took his hand.

Her vanilla musk teased his senses, along with the current that sizzled between them as he clasped her hand in his. He wished he wasn't on duty so he could make things a little more personal between them. "A most definite pleasure, Rylie Thorn."

As though remembering why she was there in the first place, the little spitfire pulled her hand from his and stepped back. "This bunch of truck thefts up and down the border, it's gone on long enough—especially here."

Clay nodded as he hooked his thumbs in his pockets. "You're telling me."

"Well, what do you intend to do about it?" Rylie put her hands on her hips, that fiery glint back in her eyes. "We just lost all of our functioning ranch trucks. New Fords, tricked out just like the hands wanted—and my personal vehicle, too. We're one of the smaller ranches in the area, and that's something we sure as hell can't afford."

Frustration at their inability to track the bastards down was a fire in Clay's gut. "Believe me, we're putting everything and everyone we can on it."

"Obviously, that's not good enough." Rylie raised her chin. "What's it been? Six weeks since the first truck went missing? I know they end up across the border where you can't do squat to get them back—but by God, they have to get from here to there. Somebody's running point right here in Douglas."

Clay ran a hand over his mustache. "I know it's not what you want to hear, but we're working on it."

"Well, that's just *great*." Her pretty eyes narrowed even more, and he wondered if she might throw a few sparks. "You know that bastard Francisco Guerrero's got a hand in this somewhere. Why don't you have him and his expensive hat down here right now, interrogating him?"

Clay kept his polite smile in place, not wanting the woman to see his sudden unease. Guerrero. That oily bastard was a big fish—and big trouble. He didn't want her making noise that might get her in trouble with Guerrero's thugs. Clay had a plan to bring down Douglas's own personal crime lord when he could get enough evidence—and Rylie Thorn getting tortured to death by pissed-off goons didn't fit into that plan.

Clay gestured toward the office's front desk. In his most placating tone, he said, "Why don't you file a report about your trucks, Ms. Thorn? I'll put your case at the top of my list."

The little wildcat glared at him. She didn't spit, but she didn't kill him, either. That had to be a win. After a second or two of stripping him down with those hot eyes, she spun and marched out of the control room.

The natural sway of her slim hips damn near killed him.

She paused at the front desk long enough to snarl, "My trucks got stolen. Send somebody out." Then she headed out the front door, muttering something about, "Damn bureaucrats. If you won't investigate, I'll just do it myself."

Clay shifted his position, trying to alleviate the new ache in his body.

What that woman just did to him, it wasn't natural.

Or maybe it was the most natural thing in the world.

Looked like he'd have to pay a visit to the Thorn Ranch.

He stood for another few seconds as the fog in his mind cleared—then he realized what she'd said as she slammed the door.

If you won't investigate, I'll just do it myself.

In the movies, when cops said, "I've got a bad feeling about this," it was time to cue the scary music.

Bad feeling didn't cover the wave of instinct that hit Clay Wayland.

Do it myself . . .

He thought about the little spitfire, and about Francisco Guerrero. She thought the drug lord was guilty—and Clay had a pretty good idea Rylie Thorn thought she was ten feet tall and bullet-proof, too.

That sealed it.

"Ah, shit." He grabbed his hat and headed out the door, barking orders at everyone standing in the office.

Chapter 2

The brakes on Rylie's old heap of a truck squealed as she stomped them right in front of the big display window at Arizona Motors South. She frowned as new clouds of smoke rolled out of the engine, and frowned harder when the truck let off belches and growls when she shut down the struggling engine.

She wiped sweat off her forehead with her hand and glanced around. Glossy high-dollar pickups for sale all around her, new and used, check. Big honking American flag and perpetual striped SALE! tent, check. Wide-eyed salesmen lying on the showroom floor with heads covered because they were convinced she was about to drive the behemoth right through their gilded showroom window—check, check, and check.

She got out of the truck, slammed the rusty, squeaking door, and stalked straight toward the entrance to the car lot's showroom, heading for the one man who'd had the guts to keep standing when she barreled in.

That hat. She'd met him several times at local events for

ranchers—rodeos and dances, that sort of thing. He was big on "supporting his community," or so he liked to pretend. Even if she hadn't been forced to shake his hand a dozen times, she'd know him anywhere just because of that stupid hat. It was an O'Farrell, a Cheyenne Pinch, black—pure beaver with a beaded edge.

I could sell the damned thing on eBay and pay my hands and the ranch expenses for a month.

Francisco Guerrero actually smiled at her when she opened the glass doors and marched onto his fancy adobe tile floor. His blacker-than-black hair peeked out from beneath his overpriced headgear, and his dark eyes appraised her with something like respectful amusement as she approached him. He had on a black silk suit, no doubt Armani, and diamonds twinkled in his cuffs, his ears, and from a diamond ring on his pinky.

Rylie pulled up short a foot or two away from him, aware of chicken-shit salesmen scrambling to their feet. Guerrero dismissed them with a quick wave of his fingers, all the while smiling at her like a cat eying a sweet bowl of cream.

Rylie felt her frown deepen to epic proportions. *It'd be a lot easier to kill the bastard if he didn't look like a movie star doing charity work for orphans.*

"Ms. Thorn. Wonderful to see you again." His gaze flicked to the ancient, battered, and smoking truck marring the landscape of his dealership, then back to her. "I can assure you, you've come to the right place to replace that eyesore."

Oh, how she'd love to slap that smile right off of Guerrero's too-handsome face. "The rest of my trucks were stolen last night. All the good ones."

"Sorry to hear that." Guerrero's smile faded. "Do the police have any leads?"

"Would I be here if they did?" Rylie gestured at the lavish surroundings. "I don't get it, Francis." She emphasized the bastardization of his given name, hoping to irk him. "You have all this and more money than God himself, but you still want more? You have to shake down ranchers barely making it to line your pockets and to buy your stupid hats and diamonds?"

His dark eyes narrowed, all hints of his megawatt smile gone now. "You think *I* stole your trucks?"

"Hell, yes!" She propped her hands on her hips and kept her eyes fixed on his. "You had something to do with it, I'm sure."

Rylie expected something along the lines of denials, threats, or getting tossed out of the dealership on her ass. She didn't expect Guerrero to throw back his head and laugh like she just told him the best joke ever. The sound seemed to bounce off the shiny showroom trucks and cars, echoing against the vaulted ceiling.

She glared at him, ignoring a handful of vehicles pulling up outside. At the very least, she might cost the arrogant jerk a few sales, right? Not that he seemed concerned, even a little bit.

She hated to admit it, but the longer he laughed, the sillier she felt. He was so relaxed, seemingly so impossible to offend. Almost like a man who really didn't have anything to hide—at least not about the trucks.

When Guerrero finally finished his belly-guffaws, she did her best to keep hold of the menacing rage she felt when she first drove up to the dealership. "I'll take that for a denial: 'I swear, Ms. Thorn,

I don't know a thing about all your pretty trucks—and half the pretty trucks in Douglas—going missing.'"

Guerrero let out another chuckle, then raised his right hand. In the smoothest, sexiest voice she'd ever heard him manage, he said, "I swear, Ms. Thorn, I don't know a thing about all your pretty trucks."

He was playing with her. Had to be. No way he was clean on these thefts. Douglas didn't have an abundance of criminals, so who else would it be? "What kind of crime lord are you?" Rylie grumbled. "I thought you assholes knew everything about what went down in your territory."

Sunlight glinted through the showroom window as people moved around outside. Rylie was glad humans were in close proximity, because Guerrero's expression finally changed from lamb to wolf. Pissed-off wolf.

Werewolf, maybe?

Uh-oh.

"Crime lord." His voice came out low and cool, and his new smile was anything but friendly. "That's a rude thing to say to a successful businessman who gives back to his community at every available opportunity."

Rylie had a moment to think that his accent got worse when he was furious, and another moment to wonder what a man like Guerrero did when he got enraged and couldn't just shoot the person who ticked him off.

Maybe she should have thought this through another five seconds.

Guerrero flexed his fingers but kept his body relaxed. "Such insults, they're beneath a beautiful woman."

For another handful of long moments, Rylie was sure the man was about to hit her. A knot tied tight in her belly and she stood very still, ready to do whatever she had to do to defend herself, but Guerrero never raised his hand or made any aggressive move.

Unsmiling, but obviously regaining control of himself, Guerrero said, "May I show you a truck, Ms. Thorn? I'd be happy to loan you one of our showroom prizes at no charge until your insurance company settles with you."

Rylie was just about to tell the slick bastard exactly what he could do with his showroom trucks when the glass door opened and she found herself facing Guerrero and the tall, handsome sheriff, Clay Wayland.

The sight of him took her breath away all over again. He seemed to tower over Guerrero, but his gaze was fixed firmly on her—and he looked worried.

She guessed she should give the man a few points for figuring out she planned to have a word with Guerrero, and extra points for worrying about that enough to show up and make sure she hadn't done any real damage.

For some reason, she couldn't hold the sheriff's gaze.

Like, maybe you just made a total fool of yourself and him, too?

What had she been thinking? That a major player in organized crime would just roll right over and confess because she challenged him?

Driving the wreck had given her heat stroke, or something. Or maybe it was the gorgeous new sheriff that had addled her mind so completely.

"Sheriff Wayland." Guerrero nodded at his new guest. "I haven't seen you since the Christmas party at Navaeh's Bed-and-Breakfast in Bisbee."

Rylie winced. Every rancher in Douglas was supposed to attend that charity dinner, but she'd blown it off this last year. She had to. Not enough money to buy a ticket, much less afford any of the drinks. Everybody in town knew it, too, and Guerrero probably knew his little jab had struck home. He didn't so much as glance at her to gloat over it.

"Mr. Guerrero." Clay Wayland's deep voice boomed through the big showroom, sending chills up and down Rylie's spine. "Is, ah, everything okay here?"

Guerrero's expression turned patient, even long-suffering, and Rylie had to work not to clench her fists. "Ms. Thorn and I were just discussing a loan of a vehicle for her until her insurance settles. I hope you'll find the people responsible for robbing our local ranchers. Times are hard enough without them losing property they'll have difficulty replacing."

Clay said nothing. The lines of his face stayed tight, and his green eyes seemed way too intense as he glanced from Rylie to Guerrero.

Rylie had no words. This level of blow-up-in-her-face hadn't been in the plans when she motored onto the car lot. All she could do was stand there and look at the fancy showroom trucks, the ceiling, the adobe floor tiles—anything but either man in the room.

"You're right, of course, Ms. Thorn. I should do more than I have to help with this local crisis." Guerrero relaxed completely again, falling back into his affable posture and firing up his smile. "Sheriff, please inform the theft victims that Arizona Motors South is happy to arrange rental vehicles, new or used, for any Douglas rancher hit by these thefts. Five dollars per day, and we'll cover the first tank of gas."

Clay Wayland's eyebrows shot up.

Rylie's did, too.

Before she could recover, Guerrero gazed at her like a saint waiting for approval from God. He looked so innocent she wanted to throw up on his pricey hat and his shiny black boots, too. "Does that help your trust level, Ms. Thorn, me taking a loss like that on a daily basis?"

No. Rylie wanted to tell Guerrero off all over again, but she was afraid he'd take back the offer, and her friends and neighbors would suffer.

"Yes," she made herself say. Damn, but that felt like pulling a tooth with no anesthetic, never mind the sweet smile she felt obligated to tack on to the end of the lie.

The worst part was, Guerrero wasn't quite finished yet. "Leave it to Ms. Thorn to remind me of my civic duties, but to refuse my charity herself. Are you certain you won't let me send you out of here in something other than *that*?"

He pointed to the wreck still taking center stage outside his showroom window.

"Thanks, but no." Rylie kept her sweet smile pasted on her face, hoping he could pick up the hefty dose of fuck-you behind all the teeth she showed. "Just help out the other ranchers who have taken hits. That's good for now."

"Fine." He gave her a little bow. "Come back any time. Lovely women are always welcome in my showroom, Ms. Thorn."

Clay Wayland's expression darkened, but Rylie could tell he didn't know what to say any more than she did.

Holding her head up and keeping her chin forward, she managed to make it to the door without ever looking at Guerrero or Clay Wayland in the face again. When she got outside, she realized she'd been sweating in the showroom. So much for bold investigative techniques.

At least the heap had the good graces to let her in and start on the third or fourth try. Somehow, she managed not to hit any of the bright, shiny trucks as she hiccuped and bucked out of the lot, heading for the safer ground of home.

Chapter 3

Rylie checked the grandfather clock in the hallway. Nearing sunset. She needed to change into her jeans, grab a sweater, and do a quick walk of her inner boundary. Damned if the truck-stealing assholes would get the wreck, or the few cars the hands kept stored in the back of the barn.

As for the Guerrero debacle earlier today—never mind. Just never mind. She wouldn't be thinking about that, or how incredibly sexy the sheriff's green eyes had been, or what he probably thought of her right about now. The good thing about honest hard work was, it got your mind off all kinds of troubles.

Wood floorboards creaked under her bare feet as she hurried to her bedroom. The old ranch house smelled of dust, lemon oil, and the single-serving lasagna she'd nuked in the microwave earlier. Unlike the modern MacKenna ranch house down the road, Rylie's home was well over a century old and looked every bit of it. But it was home and people had to stand up for home. Her mother should have, and as for her father . . . Well, that bastard wouldn't have known home if it had bit his ass cheek and given him a great, big friendly shake.

When she reached her room, she closed the door in case her older brother Levi happened to come home early. The two had been running the ranch together since Levi got back from his stint in the army, and their father and his wife—number six—had been killed in a car accident, some ten years ago.

And of course they hadn't seen their "real" mother since they were in elementary school. The woman had run off with a muscle-bound Mr. Arizona. Apparently that fling hadn't lasted, but good old Mom had enjoyed her freedom too much to get around to coming back home.

Rylie pulled her pocketknife out and tossed it on her chest of drawers. She shimmied out of her jeans, her thoughts turning to the only person who'd even been close to being like a mom to her. Mrs. Karchner, who'd given Rylie that pocketknife, used to own the ranch down the road from the Thorns. Mrs. Karchner had been the one stable person in Rylie's wild youth. But the woman passed away a few years ago, breaking Rylie's heart.

She sighed as she yanked her T-shirt over her head and tossed it onto the bed. She sure missed that woman.

After growing up in a broken family and witnessing too many failed marriages, Rylie didn't believe in commitment. But she sure as hell believed in having as much fun as possible with the opposite sex.

Maybe she was too much like her mother.

Forcing the thoughts from her mind, Rylie removed her bra and hot pink panties and then pulled on her softest pair of work jeans. Stupid things had holes just about everywhere, but she couldn't give them up. She didn't bother with panties, enjoying the soft scrub of cotton against her bare skin. She loved the feeling of being naked in these jeans, and what the hell? It would make the walk more exciting.

Not that she needed exciting. Since she set eyes on Clay Wayland this morning, she'd had a hard time getting away from the whole excitement thing. Too bad she'd been pissed about the stolen trucks when she met that sex god of a cowboy, and too bad she'd made an ass of herself flying off half-cocked over Guerrero. Or she'd have been tempted to jump the man. Well, for now she was putting aside any thought of truck theft, money woes, and lack of a man with a physique as pleasing as the sheriff's.

She had a ranch to protect. It wasn't like anybody would do it for her.

Once she had put on her leather moccasins, white T-shirt, and favorite blue sweater, Rylie slipped into the moonlit night that smelled crisp and clean from the rains of the past couple of days. Her heart beat a little faster as she picked her way through the tumbleweeds and mesquite bushes, walking the fence row, and squinting at any lump or bump that looked out of place.

The thieves could have come in from the east. That was her weakest flank. Or maybe they came from the south, straight up from the border, or from the west. Guerrero's men—and she still thought it had to be Guerrero—they'd have some preplanned route to get the trucks over the border as quickly and quietly as possible.

"Guerrero's a snake no matter how he acts in public," she grumbled to herself. "A scum with a Cornell degree, fancy manners, and a front business of auto dealerships all over Cochise County. Why the hell did he have to take my trucks? It's not like he hasn't got thousands."

But Rylie knew Guerrero was all about money and building power, and putting on a good public face with all of his charity work. He'd shown up in the Douglas-Bisbee area three or four years ago, when his old man died. Problem was, Guerrero's old man was the worst drug lord to ever cross the border, and he had three mean, soulless sons to carry on his empire. Guerrero was taking over all the criminal activity in the area, and bringing his own brand of poison, too. Like the truck thefts. So why wasn't the sheriff putting a stop to it?

Rylie crammed her hand in her pocket and gripped her knife. "Yeah, like I'll be all heroic and stop Guerrero's asswipes with this little thing." She should have brought a better weapon. If she actually did find a band of thieves skulking toward her barn, what was she going to do—offer to cut twine for them?

She peeled off the main boundary path and headed toward the cabin at the back of the ranch. Her new foreman, Brad Taylor, technically wasn't allowed to carry weapons since he was on probation from some nasty business last year that really wasn't his fault. The cabin was hers, though, along with the decorations: three rifles hung above the fireplace. They were meant to control coyotes, but they'd work just as well on truck thieves.

Her moccasins made no sound as she stole along the slightly muddy path to the cabin, moving as fast as she could without running. She had loved to play in the old cabin when she was a kid, and had kept the place in decent shape over the years as a kind of getaway when she wanted some time alone. When Brad had asked to use the cabin after she hired him, she'd thought it was a good call.

Tumbleweeds scraped her ankles just above her moccasins.

Yeah, she'd heard a few rumors about Brad and his . . . tastes, but she didn't put much stock in rumors. So what if he liked sex, and lots of it? She did, too.

Just not with twins.

Even as Rylie skirted the cabin to the back, she saw Brad's truck parked outside. Good. She had her keys, but she didn't want to barge into his space without him there, even if she did own the cabin.

As she reached the cabin's corner, she heard feminine laughter from inside.

Rylie slowed. Then stopped.

"Definitely more than one female on deck," she whispered to herself as cool evening breeze found its way through the holes in her jeans. The sensation made her shiver, along with the realization of what she might see if she let herself into Brad's cabin.

Bad. Bad, bad. I'd never . . .

Her cheeks flushed. She'd never even had the slightest urge to spy on people having sex before.

Her face got hotter.

Okay, okay, that wasn't totally true.

He's probably in there with twins. Two women at the same time.

Rylie's entire body reacted to the thought. She couldn't even let herself imagine the three of them going at it—until that laughter came again. Damn, but those girls sounded like they were having a fine time.

Just a look. One look. What could that hurt? She'd check to see if Brad was, um, busy. And if he was, she'd go back to the house to get a rifle. If he hadn't started . . . entertaining his guests, she could take one of the rifles hanging over his mantel.

The wind kicked up again, cool and erotic and exciting. Her heart beat faster, then faster again.

She eased up to the back wall of the cabin, to a knothole that was just low enough that she had to bend over. Her jeans clung to her ass, and the chilly air brushed through the dozen or so holes like tickling fingers.

Just one look, Rylie told herself.

She felt the breeze tickle her again, then bent over and peeked through the hole.

And got an eyeful.

Voices floated through the night air and Spirit's ears pricked toward the sound. Clay Wayland brought the mare to a halt, and after looking around for a moment, he swung down and let the reins drop to the ground. The mare was well trained and intelligent, and wouldn't move unless Clay whistled to her.

He'd come to find Rylie Thorn, to apologize for not getting out to take her report in person sooner, and to try to get her to agree to stay far, far away from Francisco Guerrero. He'd tried to get away earlier from the sheriff's office, then gotten himself tangled in all manner of mess and let it get late—but he knew he needed to have a talk with the little spitfire before she got herself into some serious trouble.

The lights in the main house were off except for a few, and he was worried Rylie had already turned in for the night. He sure as hell wanted to see her again, but he didn't want to wake her if she was resting. One of her ranch hands could help him out with the report just the same, and he could come back in the morning to make his point about Guerrero.

Looking for excuses to come back again already, Wayland? That's kind of pathetic.

Once Clay checked his utility belt and his firearm, he holstered the gun and quietly headed toward the only lights he saw blazing, from a small cabin he could just make out in the moonlight.

The mare grunted as he left her, and she blew out breath before lowering her nose to the ground. Clay knew she was just about as tired as he was. For the past few weeks, despite what one Miss Rylie Thorn might think, he'd been investigating the rash of truck thefts that had escalated in this part of the state. As the fairly new county sheriff, Clay's reputation was riding on getting these cases solved, and getting them solved *now*.

He'd ridden just about every local ranch looking for anything he could use, any clue to who the bastards would target next. He had to get ahead of them.

He made his way through the dry grass and tumbleweeds, trying to remember what he'd read about the old cabin on the Thorn Ranch. Brad Taylor. Yeah, that was it. Taylor had listed the cabin as his address on his probation paperwork. The boy had gotten himself into a scrape trying to protect his former boss, old Bull Fenning. Not a criminal by nature, though. Taylor was out of custody and doing well. More than well, if all the legends Clay's deputies told about his partying hard and heavy with twins were true.

Clay's hand rested on his weapon's grip, his senses on high alert even though he had no reason to suspect any thieves would show up a second night in a row. Still, he couldn't help but be on the lookout for the slightest indication of danger.

The flash of white caught Clay's eye and he froze. His eyes narrowed as he watched the small figure at the back of the cabin. When she stood, light from inside the cabin shown on her face. She shook her head. Rubbed a palm across her forehead. Shook her head again.

A woman. A damn beautiful . . . and a familiar woman at that.

Clay grinned. Definitely that little spitfire of a rancher who'd come storming into his office this morning. Rylie Thorn had more than piqued his interest.

And as she bent over to peek into a hole in the wall of the cabin, Rylie's short blond hair swung forward. Her jeans outlined each of her curves, and the T-shirt and sweater she was wearing looked so soft he wanted to touch them.

Despite years of law-enforcement training and plenty of practice in keeping emotionally and physically detached from his work, Clay couldn't help but feel a stirring. He swallowed hard, as Rylie licked her lips and wrapped her arms around herself as she stared through what had to be a knothole opening into the cabin.

A wave of feminine laughter rolled out of the cabin. Then a woman's voice said, "Do that again, Brad."

Clay's grin got a whole lot bigger. The perky little blonde was a dang Peeping Tom. Or rather, a Peeping Tomasina.

His body got more tense as he watched her standing there, seemingly frozen in place by whatever she was watching.

He could just imagine.

Damn, but he had to get his mind back on his job. He had a reason to come see the hot woman in front of him, right? At the moment he didn't have a single clue what it was.

Rylie's breath caught as she watched Brad, who stood in the center of the cabin, licking Sabrina Wilson's huge nipples. Her twin sister Sasha was on her knees giving Brad all he could handle. "You're so good at giving head, sugar," Brad said, in between mouthfuls of Sabrina's breasts.

Sabrina and Sasha were identical twins with long black hair and almond-shaped brown eyes. They both had large breasts that Rylie would've killed for, along with generous curves that Rylie envied—so unlike her own petite, compact, and athletic figure. The only difference between the twins was the small mole on Sabrina's left cheek—otherwise Rylie would never be able to tell them apart.

I can't believe I'm doing this.

But it was hot. Way past hot. The fact she didn't have anybody to share it with, to relieve her tension later . . . She tried not to think about that.

Rylie moved her hands to her own breasts as she watched Brad suckle Sabrina's nipples. The woman slipped her hands into Brad's hair and cried out as he nipped her.

"More, Brad," Sabrina demanded.

Brad rumbled something low that Rylie couldn't hear.

He'd probably love it if he knew she was watching. Rylie didn't play with her ranch hands, but Brad was almost enough to tempt a girl.

Brad moved to the lone bed across the room from the peep-hole, and lay flat on his back. With a sexy grin, he motioned for the twins to join him. Sasha giggled and climbed onto the bed. She knelt between his thighs and resumed sucking while Sabrina straddled Brad, right over his mouth.

Rylie tried to stay still, tried to ignore the heat rushing across her skin, the ache between her legs, and the tingling along the back of her neck. As she watched Sabrina grinding her hips against Brad's face, Rylie wished she had a man she could turn loose with, a man who would push her, and tease her, and satisfy her all night long.

God, she was so aroused.

This is sick. You need to stop, and you need to stop right now.

But it didn't feel sick. It just felt fun and exciting.

She bit down on her lip, holding back a moan. The night smelled of piñon and sage, and she smelled her own desire. She even imagined she caught the scent of sex coming from within the cabin.

Sabrina pinched and pulled her nipples as she yelled, "Harder!"

Rylie could feel her orgasm building. Winding up inside of her, tighter and tighter.

Sabrina screamed as she hit her peak. "Yes! God, yes!"

Rylie's whole body shuddered as she watched, engrossed, almost able to feel what the women could feel as Brad worked them, stroked them, drew out their pleasure—

A hand clamped over her mouth and another around her waist.

Rylie froze, her heart pounding and her blood rushing as her dazed mind fought to figure out what the hell was happening. Her body was still trembling and a rush of fear added to the convulsions.

"You like to watch people?" a man's deep voice murmured next to her ear, a husky whisper that sent an odd thrill straight to her core.

She couldn't move. Could barely think.

"Do you?" His tone was so low, rich, and sensual that Rylie's knees went weak as she nodded. Was there something familiar about his voice?

The man's hat brushed against her hair as he moved his body closer. She caught his masculine scent along with the faint odor of mint. And when he pressed his body to hers, she felt him through his jeans, hard against her jeans, the rough of his clothes scrubbing against some of the holes.

Ohmigod. The man's erection was *huge.*

Despite the fact the man was probably a stranger, and currently had her trapped in his grip, Rylie felt a fresh round of tingles charging through her.

"Look at them." The man's voice was hoarse, like he was almost too aroused to talk. "Does that turn you on?"

Rylie's gaze went back to the threesome in the cabin and her eyes widened. Sabrina was on her hands and knees, Brad behind her.

"Now!" Sabrina cried. Brad yanked her ass toward him and slid into her.

"Would you like to be taken right now?" the stranger asked, as Brad pounded into Sabrina.

Rylie caught her breath as the man, keeping his hand over her mouth, moved his other hand down between her thighs. Even though she didn't know who had her in his grip, and even though she had *never* had sex with anyone she didn't know, Rylie was so turned on that she wanted to shout, *Yes! Take me, now!*

But the stranger didn't wait for an answer. He slid his fingers over her jeans, and she knew he had to feel the heat.

"I bet you're smooth. I like them shaved." The stranger's voice was a silken whisper as he caressed Rylie, his callused fingers exerting the perfect motion, perfect pressure, straight through the ancient fabric.

He pushed against her sex, making her swallow a moan. "I know we'd be a good fit."

A gasp rose up within Rylie at the incredible feel of his fingers working her through her jeans and his erection pressed tight against her backside.

"What do you think, little wildcat?" The man stroked harder and Rylie couldn't hold back the moan. "I bet you taste real good, too."

Rylie trembled with a hurricane of desire as the man nuzzled her neck, his mustache brushing her soft skin as he pressed his firm lips to her. She could just imagine how that mustache would tickle her thighs. Mustache . . . Who did she know who wore a mustache?

"You smell like vanilla . . . and musk." The stranger moved his lips to the hair behind her ear and she shuddered. "Good enough to eat."

From inside the cabin, Sabrina screamed with pleasure.

"My turn." Sasha lay on her back, her black hair splayed across the old bed quilt. Brad slid between her thighs and pummeled her without so much as slowing his thrust.

Wanton feelings rose and spiraled throughout Rylie, unlike anything she'd ever felt before. On and on the stranger stroked her, murmuring erotic words, until the most intense orgasm she'd ever felt exploded through her. A scream of pleasure threatened to tear from her, but the man kept his hand tight against her mouth, holding back the sound. Her body shuddered and rocked against the stranger's as he kept her pleasure going, drawing out her climax until she couldn't take anymore.

In her haze, Rylie was dimly aware that the man had released his hold on her. She braced one hand on the cabin wall, took a deep breath, and turned to look at the man who'd given her the most incredible orgasm of her life—

Only to discover he'd vanished into the night.

Gritting his teeth, Clay eased back through the darkness to where he'd left his mare. Thoughts of Rylie consumed him . . . of tasting her, driving into her, and making her scream with orgasm after orgasm.

So much for having a stern talk with her.

When Clay reached his mare, he paused to look back toward the cabin. It was too dark and too far to see if Rylie was still there. Yet somehow he knew she hadn't left. That she was looking into the night, trying to see *him.*

Damn, but he'd never get the beautiful woman out of his mind now. His brain flashed images of taking her like Brad had taken those twins. Until she screamed. Until she couldn't move. He wanted to brand her and make her his.

Hell, she probably didn't even know who he was, but in his office and at the cabin—she'd wanted him as much as he'd wanted her—there was some kind of connection between them that was *electric*. If he'd turned her around, if he'd looked her in the face and kissed her, she might have been willing. But no, he'd walked away because of an outmoded sense of chivalry and duty.

Clay's erection throbbed against his zipper, and no amount of shifting eased the pressure. Crickets chirruped and he could still hear the faint sound of voices and laughter from the trio going at it in the cabin. A cool breeze brought scents of the desert to him, and he almost imagined he smelled the woman's vanilla musk scent.

Well, hell. He wasn't going to get anywhere at this rate. Clay could barely walk straight, much less saddle up and ride.

Spirit swatted her tail against her flank, the swish of wiry hair brushing Clay's arm. He unbuckled his belt, eased his zipper down, and pulled himself out of his briefs. Imagining he was sliding into Rylie's sweet core, he stroked himself from base to tip. Yeah, he could just picture that hot little body, thighs spread wide and showing him her shaved sex.

He knew she'd be shaved. He just knew it.

While he stared into the night, toward where he'd left the woman, his motions increased as he remembered her smell, the feel of her ass pressed against him. His body tensed, and heat flooded him from his Stetson to his steel-toed boots. Clay gritted back a groan as he finally got a little relief.

Unreal.

Unbelievable.

He hadn't acted like this since he was a teenager.

Shaking his head, he slipped himself back into his briefs and fastened his jeans and belt. He wasn't sure he'd ever been that horny even when he *was* a teenager. He'd certainly never had almost-sex while on the job.

It was a definite. This woman's effect on him—it wasn't normal, but Clay wasn't the type of man who worried about things like that. He was the type of man who knew what had to be done, and took care of business.

Clay mounted Spirit and guided the mare away from the ranch and back toward where he'd left his truck and horse trailer. He may have walked away from Rylie tonight, but come tomorrow, he'd find her and stake his claim.

And next time he intended to do a lot more than feel a little heat through her jeans.

Chapter 4

The front door slammed, the reverberations rattling through the house and waking Rylie. She blinked away early-morning sunlight as wisps of her dream came back to her—of a dark stranger with a very impressive package and some talented fingers.

Her body ached at the thought of what had happened last night to inspire such an erotic dream. A tiny part of her thought she should feel properly guilty for her Peeping Tom routine and maybe even freaked out by making out with a stranger—but the rest of her said, Screw it.

It was hot.

It was fun.

Rylie might be uptight about a lot of things, but sex sooo wasn't one of them. Healthy, heated, and consensual—that's all that counted.

She smiled and stretched her limbs, the sheet sliding across her bare flesh and down to her waist, exposing her body to the cool morning air. She always slept in the nude and loved how freshly laundered linens smelled, and how they felt against her naked skin.

With a grin, Rylie bounded out of bed and snatched her robe off the hook on the back of her bedroom door. She was a morning person and rarely slept in late, but that dream had certainly been worth sleeping in for. She had needed something to help her forget about the truck thefts, and had last night ever been the ticket.

She slipped on her robe and then opened her door to head to the bathroom across the hall, her mind wandering to the memory of last night. How incredible it felt to have the stranger's muscled body pressed tight to her backside, his big hand between her thighs, his fingers moving like they knew exactly where to touch. That deep, sexy voice of his was enough to make her explode just thinking about it.

Too bad the man had pulled a vanishing act. She had a feeling he would've been one hell of a ride. His voice, though . . . Something about it had been familiar. Was he someone she knew? He had a mustache, wore jeans and a Western hat—that much she'd been able to tell. She knew a few men with mustaches—Wade Larson and a couple of Skylar MacKenna's ranch hands . . . but the voice just didn't match any of them.

Rylie shut and locked the bathroom door as she thought about how she'd instinctively trusted her mystery man. She had a natural intuition about most folks that was almost always dead-on. The one time she didn't listen to that internal voice, she came close to being raped in high school by an asshole named Reggie Parker. Thank God Levi had come to her rescue and kicked Reggie's skinny white ass.

Unfortunately, Levi had ended up in jail overnight for hitting a minor. That bastard Reggie had deserved having his face turned into hamburger. Rylie still owed her big brother for that one.

The faucet creaked and pipes groaned as Rylie ran the water in the tub, waiting for it to turn from freezing to only chilly before she jumped in. She and Levi needed to get a new water heater in the worst way, but right now most of their cash was sunk into the herd and she was going to have to shell out a bunch more to cover the cost of new trucks, whatever insurance didn't pay. If only the price of beef would go back up, they might be able to afford a thing or two. The smell of rust met her nose, the water coming out orangish-red, compliments of plumbing twice her age. New pipes would be nice, too. Hell, a new house was what they really needed.

Once the water ran clear, Rylie ditched her robe and stepped under the spray. She shivered from the burst of cold. Accustomed to rushing through her morning ice-water shower, she shampooed her hair, soaped her body, and shaved her armpits, legs, and other places in record time.

How did he know I was the shaving type? Mystery Man must have himself some good instincts.

Rylie thought about how the stranger enjoyed touching her. What would he look like? Judging by the height of his package pressed against her backside, she figured he was a good eight inches taller than her, which would put him at close to six feet.

Her body got a lot warmer despite the chill of the water on her flesh. He was big in other ways. She had definitely been able to tell that without even touching him with her hands. Ten inches, or she'd eat a pair of her own underwear. A man like that, tall and strong and well proportioned . . .

Yum.

The sound of water roared in Rylie's ears, blending with the pounding of her heart. Goose bumps sprouted on her skin, and she knew she had to get a grip and drag herself back to reality.

Reluctantly, she shut off the water and reached for a towel off the rack.

Too bad reality couldn't always be like last night.

Clay wondered why he was even trying to concentrate. Every three seconds, his mind wandered to Rylie Thorn, and once he got her in his thoughts, he couldn't get her out.

She fit in his hands like he had been born to touch her. And the way she smelled, the silk of her skin— Damn. Just, damn.

He shook his head, but that didn't help, so he took a deep breath and forced himself to stare at the file folders on the desk in front of him: "Hazard Quinn," "Sam Blalock," and "Joe Garrison." His three day-shift deputies, or more to the point, the heap of a mess he had inherited from the previous sheriff. These men had little training, even less discipline, and they had been allowed to run wild with a boss who barely showed up to work, and a superior officer, Gary Woods, who had gone about as bad as a law officer could go.

Clay glanced out his office window. Hazard Quinn was bent over a stack of papers, his too-tall dark hair sprayed in place as if he hoped he'd run into Elvis or Lyle Lovett, and be able to express his undying admiration. The boy worked hard, but he was young and he had a tendency to go off half-cocked. Then there was Sam Blalock—blond, too handsome for his own good—and that goatee, which would have to stay trimmed. Clay didn't want anybody working for him who reminded him of old church paintings of Satan. Blalock had proven himself handy at turning up information other people missed, and that was good, because Joe Garrison was hitting middle age, working on a whole lot of nothing besides his paunch. The man had a tic that made him blink until Clay could barely concentrate when he was trying to work with the guy.

"Construction projects," Clay muttered to himself. "All three of them." He closed the folders, stacked them up, and pushed them off to the side. Then he picked up a list he'd been keeping, folded it, and slipped it into his jeans pocket. He wasn't going to start thinking about Rylie Thorn again, not unless he kept sitting on his ass. The only cure for wanting a woman like he was wanting her was work, hard work, and lots more work on top of that.

He walked out into the main area and pointed to Quinn and Blalock. "You and you. Come with me. We've got a few stops to make." To Garrison, Clay said, "Hold the fort and give us a shout if you need us."

Garrison looked relieved that he wouldn't have to do much of anything, and Clay bit back a rumble of irritation. He'd lead, the young ones would follow, and before long, Garrison would either pick up his step or get on out of their way.

Clay took a squad car and had both deputies follow in another. He hadn't made an appointment, but after yesterday's little display,

Guerrero had opened the door for him to waltz back into Arizona Motors South with a semblance of a good excuse. When he pulled into the lot, he parked in a far-off spot and had Quinn and Blalock do the same.

He got out into the day's heat and motioned to both men, who stopped in front of him, alert and nervous.

Good.

They should be nervous this close to a swimming shark or a prowling wolf. Nervous might keep them both alive when things got dicey down the road.

He faced the older of the two, the one with the chin hair. "When we go in, I'm going to talk to Guerrero alone. Blalock, you keep an eye on the employees. I want to know what they do, how they seem to you."

"Yessir." Blalock bobbed his head and his goatee bounced up and down.

Clay tried not to notice. He turned to Quinn and continued with Police Work for Kindergarteners. "Guerrero's office is glassed in instead of walled off, so the view's clear. Stand off a few paces and keep an eye on Guerrero as he talks to me. Watch for anything I might not see."

"Gotcha, boss." Quinn smoothed his hair even though not a strand was out of place, couldn't possibly be out of place, and probably would snap clean off if Clay breathed on it too hard. He wasn't sure he could trust a man who used hair spray, but for now, he didn't have much choice.

He glanced at the sky, half hoping God would make an appearance and tell him what to do with these two, but he didn't see so much as a single cloud. The three of them entered the auto dealership, hot and nearly sun-blind, and the cool air hit Clay like a quick slap on both cheeks.

Guerrero's salesmen saw them, but didn't approach, which was fine with Clay. Blalock drifted off into the showroom just like he'd been told, and Quinn glanced at Guerrero's glass office and got busy picking his spot.

Clay headed straight for Guerrero's door, knocked, and went in when Guerrero looked up and gestured to him.

Guerrero stood, and Clay noted he was dressed all in black, just like the day before, except for his red tie. Maybe he was trying to make black silk a trademark.

Maybe he'd get on good with Hair-spray Boy out in the showroom.

He slipped the list out of his jeans with his left hand and made himself shake Guerrero's proffered hand with his right.

"I brought a list of victims who would like to take you up on your rental offer."

"Excellent." Guerrero showed Clay to a leather seat in front of his desk, then sat in his rolling wing chair. "I'll have my men call and make appointments for these people."

He placed the list on his desk, smoothing out the wrinkles, and he gave Clay his best canned smile.

Clay waited for the other shoe to drop, the casual mention of how much it might cost the people for insurance, or fees, or some crap like that. Guys like Guerrero didn't give something for nothing.

His low opinion must have showed on his face, because Guerrero's smile slipped away and he said, "You have something else on your mind, Sheriff?"

What the hell. Clay leaned back in his leather chair. *Got to start somewhere with everybody in this town, him included.* "Mr. Guerrero, you and I don't know each other very well. I've got files and rumors and a handful of personal impressions—not much to go on."

Guerrero folded his hands on his desk. He didn't look exactly wary, but he wasn't all open-and-friendly, either. "And?"

"And you don't strike me as a man who'd waste his time on small-time truck thefts. High risk, minimal payoff."

Guerrero went silent for a few seconds, studying Clay with unreadable black eyes. Clay couldn't be sure, but he thought the man might be weighing his options, choosing his next statement carefully.

What came out was, "I'm not a thief, Mr. Wayland. I'm a businessman."

"So I've heard." Talking points, just like a damned politician. "And so you keep saying to anyone who'll listen."

The muscles in Guerrero's face twitched. Again, he studied Clay like he was trying to choose the right words, or figure the right course of action.

He probably had some kind of deal with my predecessor. Hope he won't be damned stupid enough to approach me with that kind of bullshit.

Clay kept his expression amiable enough, but let his eyes speak his mind for him.

"My family has many business interests," Guerrero said, speaking more slowly than usual. "At times, my interests align with theirs, primarily when I have no choice. Mostly, I sell cars, Sheriff Wayland."

This guy was a true piece of work. Was he trying to say he didn't want to play ball with his brothers, that he didn't want a share of the Guerrero empire?

If so, he was lying through his shiny teeth.

Clay nodded. Whatever. For now, he'd play along. At least he hadn't started talking bribes or posturing like a bad imitation of the Godfather—that was a plus.

Clay got up to make his exit, and Guerrero stood, displaying, as usual, his impeccable manners. At the door, Clay made a split-second decision, stopped, turned back to Guerrero, and left him with, "If you happen on any information that might help our local ranchers, I'd appreciate hearing about it."

He stopped short of saying he'd owe the creep a favor. Guerrero wasn't a man to be indebted to, not for any reason, no matter what kind of grand con he was trying to run on Douglas.

Guerrero seemed to hear what he said, and what he didn't say. "I'll ask around, but I doubt I'll find out anything of interest to you."

Clay put his hand on the office door again, and Guerrero added, "Whoever is doing this, I'd say he was desperate for fast cash. Like you mentioned—high risk, little payoff."

Clay gave the man a nod, then left his office. He approached Quinn, who was shifting from foot to foot and actually did have a hair out of place. Two hairs. Maybe three.

"How did he seem to you, Quinn?"

"Relaxed," the kid said. "It didn't look like an act."

Miracles do happen. "That was my take."

Blalock joined them near the showroom door, and as they stepped back out into the heat, he said, "The salesmen were all business. They're well trained, I guess."

"Or just not concerned," Clay suggested.

They walked in silence back to the squad cars, and as Clay got to his door, Quinn said, "Are you thinking Guerrero's not involved?"

Clay shrugged. "Anything's possible."

"If it's a crime and it involves money, he's got his hand in it somewhere," Blalock said. "I mean, that's my opinion. Sir."

The younger man glanced at the ground, obviously anxious about offending his new boss. Quinn held his peace, but he glared back through the plate-glass window and nodded.

"Pisses me off, sir," Quinn muttered, "that we can't take them down when we know they're dirty. He's got blood on his hands."

"His family does," Clay said. "As for him, sooner or later, we'll sweep up all the trash in this town. Blalock, hook up with our contacts at ICE and with the DEA. Stay on Guerrero, but keep your distance—and keep ICE and DEA in the loop."

As Blalock nodded, looking like a kid with a brand-new toy to play with, Clay got in his car. Less than a minute later, his thoughts went straight back to Rylie Thorn.

It was late afternoon by the time Rylie was close to finishing her daily chores in the barn behind the old ranch house. The sun hung low over the Mule Mountains and the air smelled of fall, mixed with barn smells of dust, manure, and alfalfa hay.

Humming softly to herself, Rylie raked out Sassafras's stall. Sass was a dappled Appaloosa mare that more than lived up to her name, but to Rylie the ten-year-old horse was like a member of the family. Sass had distinctive cream-colored knee-high stockings on her front legs, but her back legs were solid chocolate brown, as was most of her coat where she didn't have cream spots. A diamond blaze was on her sleek muzzle, and she had a mischievous spark in her intelligent brown eyes.

Rylie loved to ride whenever she got the chance. It had been her favorite activity as she was growing up, her way to escape the world and her screwed up family life. She'd done pretty well in rodeo competitions, even beating Skylar MacKenna a few times in barrel racing.

A couple of stalls down from Sass was Shadow Warrior, a champion stallion they'd had for eight years. They'd had to sell the rest of their horses when things got tough and they couldn't afford the feed or maintenance any longer. They used Warrior primarily for stud service, as a way to add a little cash to their income. And Sass, well, there was no way in hell Rylie would ever let her go.

The mare hung her head over the side of the next stall and lipped Rylie's short blond hair. "Cut that out." She grinned and shooed Sass away with a playful pat on the mare's muzzle. Sass whickered and tossed her head, acting for all the world like she was laughing at Rylie.

The entire morning, all Rylie had been able to think about was the stranger from last night. She had never let *any* man under her skin, and it was starting to irk her that she couldn't get one little sorta-sexual encounter off her mind.

It was different. It was a rush. But, really. All day, circling around the same guy in her head?

It had to be curiosity. Yeah, that was it. She couldn't stop wondering what it might be like to actually have sex with the man. The man who had a voice so deep and sensual it sent shivers through her just thinking about it.

After Rylie's experience with the stranger, even Luke Denver, Skylar MacKenna's ranch foreman, didn't seem half as intriguing as before—and Luke was one hot cowboy, with an incredibly sexy drawl. Rylie had been flirting with Luke since she met him, but he'd kept his distance, and now he'd gotten married off to Skylar's little sister and he was about to take off on a long-delayed honeymoon.

Tingles skittered along Rylie's spine and she stopped raking when the thought of another incredible hunk crossed her mind.

It couldn't have been *him.* Could it?

Yesterday, when she'd met Clay Wayland, both before *and* after making an ass of herself, she'd just about melted the instant she'd laid eyes on him. She hadn't been able to speak at first, she'd been so totally captured by lust. He had the most amazing crystalline green eyes, an incredibly deep and thrilling voice, and the sexiest mustache . . .

Dogs barking and the sound of a truck driving up to the ranch jerked Rylie from her fantasizing. She propped the rake up against the stall door, pulled off her leather work gloves, and tossed them onto a hay bale. Wiping her hands on her jeans, she stomped her boots on the hard-packed dirt floor to kick loose some of the manure.

"Be right back, girl." Rylie patted Sass's neck and headed toward the open barn door.

She paused in the shadows, and her heart rate picked up when she saw a truck with the county sheriff's logo park in her front yard. And then a warm flush stole over her as that fine-looking lawman climbed out of it. . . .

Clay Wayland.

Oh. My. God.

It couldn't have been him last night.

Damn—it had to be.

As she watched the sheriff stride from the truck, Rylie tugged on her ear, a nervous habit she'd had since she was a child. Sheriff Wayland walked up to Levi, who was standing in front of the house.

The two knew each other in passing, she remembered, because Wayland had asked Levi to use his experience from Special Forces and his contacts at the U.S. Marshals to track down somebody for him a few months ago. Levi hadn't been able to find the person, but Wayland had seemed grateful for the favor.

Levi smiled and shook hands with Wayland, and Rylie wished she was closer so that she could hear what they had to say. If she wasn't so sweaty and didn't smell like the barn, she would have strolled right out. She wanted more of what she knew that sheriff could give her.

That lawman was one hot hunk of male. Tall, broad shoulders, narrow hips, and a tight ass. She had a side view of him, and couldn't tell what color his hair was because of his Stetson, but he had a sexy sable mustache and nice big hands. She liked a man with big—

As if aware of her, Wayland looked straight to where she was hidden in the shadows. The world stopped on its axis, and for one long moment, she all but forgot how to breathe.

Prickling erupted at Rylie's nape and the fine hairs stood up on her arms.

He couldn't see her, could he?

Her heart beat faster as his eyes seemed to lock with hers. But then he turned back to Levi and continued talking like nothing strange had just happened.

Nothing *had* happened. Surely it was just her desire and thoughts of what happened last night that was making her crazy.

Rylie eased back into the barn, her skin tingling. Her normal I-don't-give-a-damn-what-anyone-thinks attitude had suddenly taken a hike. She was sweaty, probably had dirt streaked across her face, and smelled like a horse—not to mention the horseshit. As much as she was dying to get to know that sexy lawman, now was *not* the right time.

Biting her bottom lip, Rylie yanked on her gloves and set back to work, determined not to sneak another peek at the gorgeous man outside.

Sass whickered and moved her head up and down in a kind of horsey nod, as though telling Rylie she should go out and see him anyway.

Rylie glared at her. "What do you know?" she muttered. "You're just a horse."

In response, Sass snorted and blew snot all over Rylie's shirt.

"Brat." Rylie swiped at it with her gloves and managed to wipe the worst of it off. "See if you get your sugar lump later."

There she was.

Clay knew it deep in his gut that Rylie was there as soon as he'd driven up to the Thorn Ranch. While he talked to Levi Thorn about the truck thefts and the report he had filed this morning after getting Levi to fax him the vehicle information, Clay's instincts had kicked in. And then he'd *felt* Rylie watching him from the barn.

He pushed up the brim of his hat and turned his attention back to Levi. "Anything else unusual happen on your property that you're aware of?" Clay asked, watching Levi for any sign of recognition or discomfort at the questioning. "Anything at all?"

"Other than losing fifteen head of cattle during the rustling mess from last year?" Levi shook his head, his manner calm and amiable. "Nothing more than the fence being cut a couple of times. Between the Flying M and our ranch. Luke Denver, the foreman over at Flying M, he's riding the line just like me, but he's getting ready to leave town for his honeymoon.

"Too damned bad we haven't been able to catch the bastards in action," Levi continued. "Maybe that's where they came through to get at the trucks, but I didn't see any tire tracks around there when I went out this morning."

Clay nodded. "Mind if I talk with your sister?"

With a shrug, Levi jerked his thumb in the direction of the barn. "Ry's probably working with her Appaloosa."

After thanking Levi and shaking the man's hand again, Clay strode toward the barn. Blood thrummed in his veins, the same feeling he always got when he was close to solving a case.

For more than ten years he'd been a street cop and then a detective with the Tucson Police Department. He'd served with TPD from the time he was a rookie until he'd decided to move to the southeastern corner of Arizona to take over as Sierra Vista's chief of police, some six years ago.

Needing a new challenge, Clay had decided to run for Cochise County Sheriff and the previous fall he had beat out the troubled incumbent by a hefty margin. The papers were making a big deal over the truck thefts, and Clay was determined to seek out the culprits and lock the bastards up.

In a few strides, he made it to the open barn door. Even before he walked into the barn, Clay heard the sound of a rake scraping against the ground and a horse's soft whicker. When he entered, he stopped for a moment, allowing his eyes to adjust to the dimness. His gaze immediately focused on the petite blond who had her back to him and was raking out a stall.

Clay smiled and his body jerked to attention. He would recognize that fine little ass anywhere . . . even without the sexy worn-out jeans.

The Appaloosa raised its head and eyed Clay, but Rylie didn't seem to realize he was there. Just like last night.

He eased up behind her. "Hello, Rylie Thorn."

Rylie gave a small shriek and whirled around. She clenched the rake to her chest, her big brown eyes wide. "What the hell did you sneak up on me for?" She raised her chin and took a step back. "You like to have scared the crap out of me."

Damn, but she was cute, right down to the sprinkling of freckles across her nose, and Clay couldn't help but grin. "You gonna hit me with that thing?"

She glanced at the rake handle and back at him. "Depends."

Clay raised an eyebrow. "On what?"

"If you ever do that again."

As she stared up at the man, Rylie took a deep breath and tried to calm her scattered thoughts and the pounding of her heart. It *was* him last night. That incredible voice and those mesmerizing crystal green eyes . . . she was definitely in lust.

"Why don't we try this again?" His mustache twitched as he smiled and held out his hand. "It's good to see you again, Ms. Thorn."

"'Ms. Thorn'?" She propped the rake against the stall door, pulled off her gloves, and tucked them into her back pocket. "Don't you think we're a little beyond that, Sheriff Wayland?"

"Yeah." He took her hand, and damn if his touch didn't send tingles straight to where it counted. "After last night, I hope you'll just call me Clay."

His eyes swept over her, lingering on the swell of her breasts and her thin T-shirt. She didn't feel the need to wear a bra all the time, and right now she felt almost naked under his gaze.

Rylie, who had never found herself at a loss for words around a man, once again couldn't think of a thing to say, just like the first time she'd met him in his office. Her body vibrated with awareness and need, and all she wanted to do was get naked with him. *Now.*

"Well?" He released her hand and brought his fingers to her face. She felt him lightly brushing dirt away from her cheek. "What do you say?"

She leaned into the touch of his hand against her face. "Yes."

Clay cocked an eyebrow and cupped her chin with his hand. "Yes . . . what?"

"Whatever you're asking," she murmured, her eyes focused on his, "the answer's yes."

A slow, sexy smile crept over his face, and his voice dropped to that seductive pitch that made her knees weak. "If I wanted to kiss you, that'd be all right?"

Rylie brought her hand up to the copper sheriff's star pinned to his shirt, and traced it with her finger. "Damn straight."

He moved closer, so that his muscled body was a fraction from hers, so close she could feel the heat of him through her T-shirt and jeans. "What if I said I wanted more, Rylie? Right here in the barn. You'd say yes?"

She kept her gaze locked with his as she placed her hand right on the bulge beneath his jeans, giving him his answer. He sucked in his breath as she trailed her fingernails up and down his impressive length. God, he was big, and did she *ever* want him.

Clay dropped his hand from her face as he fought to control the lust building up within him. "If you're not careful, little wildcat, I might just take you up on what you're offering."

"Oh?" Rylie's chocolate-brown eyes sparkled with sensuality. "What's stopping you?"

"Only the fact that I'm on the job." He resisted the urge to taste those sweet lips that pursed into a sexy smile. "And the fact that your brother and someone else are real close to walking in on us." He jerked his head toward the barn door to where he heard the sound of voices coming closer.

"Oh." She lowered her hand from his crotch and grinned. "Works for me."

"About that 'yes' . . ." Clay stepped away, putting some distance between them before unwelcome company arrived. "Dinner tomorrow night. I'll pick you up at seven."

She didn't even hesitate. "What should I wear?"

And neither did he. "Short skirt. Tight shirt. No underwear, if you've got the guts."

Dear God.

Rylie shivered as Clay moved away from her to the barn door to talk with Levi and the man she had formerly lusted over, Luke Denver, the Flying M Ranch foreman. Rylie couldn't help but enjoy the view as she watched the gorgeous sheriff talk with Luke and Levi. Luke really was an example of prime U.S. male with dark brown hair, blue eyes that could make a woman beg, a Bruce Willis adorable grin, and a sexy drawl.

Yet now after she'd met Clay Wayland, Rylie didn't even feel a twinge of lust for Luke anymore. Well, that was strange. She'd never had any problem maintaining multiple lustings before.

"Some assholes tried to steal Skylar MacKenna's truck," Luke was saying to Clay. "Damn near caught the bastards red-handed, but they got away."

Rylie's attention snapped from thoughts of the sheriff to concern for her friend and her friend's ranch. She walked up to the men, feeling like a pixie in the land of the giants. "Is Skylar all right?"

Luke looked down at Rylie and gave her that grin of his that used to make her knees feel like gelatin. "Hey there, Rylie." His friendly smile vanished as he answered her question. "Yeah, Skylar's fine. She's not even here. But that's the second attempt this week on our vehicles. We're setting up cameras and doing guard duty in shifts."

He turned back to Levi and Clay. "Skylar left town for a week with her new husband Zack Hunter, and my wife Trinity went with them to do a little shopping in Bisbee, to get some clothes for our honeymoon. My thinking is that the thieves knew they were out of town, so that's why they picked last night to strike, not counting on me being around."

"Their trip sure was suddenlike," Clay murmured.

Levi shook his head, laughter in his blue eyes. "Well, if you'd seen those two before they left . . . my guess is they've found themselves a hotel room and won't be seeing daylight for a while. I don't know what Trinity'll be doing with herself."

Luke snickered. "Spending lots of money on clothes I won't let her wear longer than five minutes."

Rylie had to laugh, too. The last time she'd seen Skylar was at dinner a couple of nights ago, and Zack couldn't keep his eyes off of her even though they were sneaking up on their six-month anniversary.

When the two lovebirds couldn't stand it any longer, Levi, Luke, Trinity, and Rylie had been left alone to finish dinner and clean up the mess—not that anyone complained. The men were more than happy to polish off every bite of the enchiladas.

Later, Skylar had called briefly to say that she and Zack were going on a little trip to Bisbee, with Trinity tagging along to hit the shops, and she'd call when they returned.

Clay smiled, but his expression went serious again. "So there's a good chance that thieves are people who hang around enough to know what's going on at the ranch."

With a nod, Luke replied, "Yeah. But the question remains: is this Guerrero or some other shithead with a plan?"

The mention of Guerrero's name turned Clay's smile to a frown. He cut a quick look at Rylie, and she felt it like an ominous warning.

He's worried I'm going to act like an idiot again.

She wondered if she should be offended, then blew it off. It was kind of cute, how he was concerned about her. Clay Wayland would learn soon enough that she could take care of herself. In fact, she might enjoy teaching him.

"Sooner or later, Guerrero will make a mistake big enough to take him down." Levi took off his Western hat and ran a hand through his thick blond hair. "His boys will screw up and leave a trail, and we'll get them all."

Luke's scowl came close to matching Clay's. "They didn't screw up last night. I couldn't even follow their tracks more than a mile. They know the land, and they know what they're doing—and what law enforcement might look for and find."

"Why don't I head over to the MacKenna ranch with you?"

Clay stroked his hand over his mustache and Rylie imagined what it would feel like to have that hand stroking her instead. "I'd like to check everything out myself."

Luke said, "Suit yourself. Check out whatever you want, but I've given it a real thorough once-over."

Check out whatever you want. Rylie studied Sheriff God-bod. *No shit. Can't wait to check out every inch of that.*

Clay's eyes met Rylie's and for a moment she was sure he'd read her mind. He smiled and tipped his hat. "See you later, Rylie Thorn."

Chapter 5

"Finally? Seriously?" Rylie nearly dropped the phone onto the kitchen floor in mock surprise.

"I know, I know." The excitement in Skylar's voice was unmistakable. "We know it's late for a reception, but we got married so fast in such a small ceremony; it's time to celebrate with all of our friends."

Rylie relaxed against a counter, unable to stop grinning. Skylar sounded so giddy and happy. "So when? Where?"

"We haven't decided on a place or day yet. I just wanted to know you'd be on board. It wouldn't be a party unless you showed up."

Rylie was sure she heard Zack in the background, murmuring something like "Party with me. *I'm* the desperado."

Rylie pulled her pocketknife from her jeans and flicked it open and closed. Open and closed. "Honey, if it's a party, you know I'll be there. It's just . . . I still can't get used to the idea that you're *married*."

"*Zack.* Not now." Skylar giggled and Rylie rolled her eyes, imagining the sickly sweet, almost-newlywed crap going on at the other end of the line. "I know what you mean," Skylar continued into the phone, "I keep thinking I'll get used to it too, but so far it's still one giant head-rush."

Even though she was dead-set against marriage, Rylie crammed her pocketknife in her jeans and tried to muster up joy for her friend who sounded so happy, and put a smile in her voice. "Tell that cowboy he'd better take good care of you, or I'll kick his ass."

"I'll let him know." Laughter bubbled up from Skylar. "What do you think about our having the reception next Saturday? We could have a barbeque and dance here at the ranch. Trinity will already be gone, but I think the timing would work for everybody else."

"Sounds perfect." Rylie held the phone with one hand and tugged at her earlobe with her other as she did her best to put some enthusiasm into her voice. "And don't worry about me and all my rules against marriage. You know I wouldn't miss it. I'd never let you down, Skylar."

"Great. Be here at noon." Skylar sighed, a sound of contentment. She was so damn happy that Rylie couldn't help but feel pleasure for her friend. "What's new with you, sweet pea?"

Rylie's body warmed at the mere thought of the sheriff.

"I'm going out tomorrow night with Clay Wayland," she said aloud.

"The sheriff?" Skylar's voice perked up. "I've met him—talk about one hell of a sexy man. I just knew you'd find him hot. Promise to give me all the juicy details."

"Don't I always?" Rylie's smile was wistful. Their nightlong girl gabfests had come to an abrupt end with Skylar's getting shackled. She didn't see them cranking back up anytime soon. That's what marriage did to a person. Isolated them. Took them away from their friends and family. It started out all sweetness, but it would end with yelling and distance and pain.

After they said their good-byes, Rylie punched the phone off and set it on the countertop.

Married. What the hell had Skylar been thinking when she eloped last October? Rylie shook her head. It had been good to hear Skylar's excitement all these months, but Rylie just hoped her friend had made the right decision and would be happy next year and the year after that. Skylar deserved that and more.

But as far as Rylie was concerned, marriage was a mistake she was damn sure she would *never* make. Happily ever after was a long damned time, and till-death-us-do-part, that was too much to even consider.

She did her best to shake off the trapped feeling she got whenever she thought about marriage, then headed out to saddle Sass for a quick ride of the ranch boundaries.

Less than half an hour later, she and Sass moved along the fence line, blue sky stretching endlessly above them and wavy thick grass shimmering in a hot breeze. The day smelled like fertile ground, leather, and horse, and that was fine by Rylie. Riding was the ultimate freedom, and riding her own stretch, land that she'd worked and suffered for—nothing beat that.

Except maybe wild sex with a certain larger-than-life sheriff . . .

Rylie sighed and gave Sass's reins a gentle tug, turning toward the back quarter of the ranch. She so didn't need to go there, back to obsessing about Clay, but it was hard to avoid. The ranch's farthest corner at the base of the Chiricahua Mountains seemed so peaceful and quiet she didn't have much to keep her mind anywhere else.

Sass's hooves made soft *clop-clops* on the dirt path as Rylie scanned the fencing, looking for holes or tears. So far, nothing. She hadn't even seen any tracks in the dirt that didn't belong.

She rounded another corner, the hot breeze making its way over her face—

Rylie pulled Sass to a halt, and sat ramrod straight in her saddle.

She sniffed the air again, just to be sure she hadn't imagined the smell that snapped her back to full alert.

There it was. A fruity, almost bitter scent. A man's cologne, expensive, but jarring. Unpleasant.

Rylie squinted, searching the shadows around nearby brush and trees. She knew that smell. She *remembered* it. Before she could get hold of herself, images rushed at her, grabbing her mind and forcing her heart to full gallop.

Hands grabbing her . . .

Reggie's toothy leer as he held her down in the backseat of that putrid old car . . .

Torn leather digging into her shoulders, her arms as she fought him . . .

"You're gonna enjoy this, bitch. You've been asking for it . . ."

Rylie swore and ripped herself out of the past. Her fingertips flew to her cheek, which was somehow stinging from the slap Reggie gave her all those years ago. He'd ripped off her shirt, yanked down her pants, and he was working on getting his jeans off when Levi showed up.

Her heart thundered even as she reminded herself it wasn't much of a fight after that. Levi had snatched the little bastard off her and thrown him down. Reggie, proving he was stupid on top of being an asshole, got up, and then Levi really took him down. Punched him so hard Reggie probably heard little birdies tweeting in his brain for a month or two. The jerk lost a tooth, got his jaw broken, and had to eat soup through a straw for a long, long time.

Levi never should have been charged for hitting the creep. Everything got sorted out soon enough, though, and Rylie had felt even safer when Reggie pulled up stakes and left town after graduation.

Safe. Until now.

Rylie glanced around again, trying to squash the frantic worry making her muscles go tense. She hadn't imagined that smell, and she'd never known anybody but Reggie to blow that much money on cologne that turned to skunk oil the second he slathered it on in the morning.

She sniffed the air again and smelled nothing. The woods seemed as quiet and empty as ever, except—

Rylie's skin prickled all over, and her breath caught.

She felt eyes on her, somebody watching.

"Get a grip," she whispered to herself, but Sass snorted and danced. "Whoa, girl. Easy there."

The horse tugged her head against Rylie's grip, wanting rein to run, wanting to charge straight home, back to the safety of the barn and the ranch house and the hands, and somewhere on his own rounds, Levi.

This was stupid. She had a bad case of the shivers, and now she'd given them to Sass. Rylie got pissed at herself, which helped the panic until bushes rustled in the distance.

Enough. Enough!

She gave Sass the rein the horse wanted, and the Appaloosa whirled and bolted back the way they had come. Rylie ducked low to miss branches and gripped the horse hard with her calves. She kept one hand in Sass's mane and the other tight on the reins and her saddle horn. She refused to let the horse run wild, made her control the gallop—but she let Sass run. Wanted her to run.

They broke into open ground a minute or so later. Hot air blasted into Rylie's face, and sunlight flowed across her face, her eyes, turning the entire world yellow. She couldn't smell Reggie anymore, didn't feel that sense of being stared at, but her heart was pounding harder than Sass's hooves and she couldn't slow it down.

Another few seconds and she got enough sanity back to bring Sass to a trot before the mare worked up a lather. It was too hot for this kind of crap. What kind of idiot was she being?

The barn came into view, and Rylie felt twice as stupid for flipping out over nothing. She pulled Sass back again, bringing the horse to a fast walk. Somebody was riding out to meet her, and he was coming so hard his Stetson blew off and bounced across the grass. He didn't even slow down.

Levi. She could tell by the set of his shoulders and the way he controlled his horse. Nobody could ride like her brother.

It's okay, the teenage part of her brain babbled. *Levi is here. Everything will be fine now.*

"Dammit." Rylie reined Sass and swung down from her saddle, ground-tying the mare by dropping the leather straps to the dusty trail. She let out a big breath, almost as big as the horse's long, exasperated blow Sass gave her. "I do *not* need Levi or any other man to feel safe. I can take care of myself."

And she could. She'd been doing just that since she was out of high school. So why did she feel sixteen again, vulnerable and pinned, helpless against whatever was about to happen?

Levi reached her, reined, and dismounted in one fluid motion. "Ry, what the hell? You were riding like the devil himself was on your ass."

"I— Never mind." She tried to focus on Levi's blond hair, how it was mussed and hanging in his face, making him look like a kid again. "I just got spooked."

Levi frowned and looked twice as worried. "You don't spook." He glanced in the direction she'd come from. "What's back there?"

Rylie rolled her eyes at her own idiocy and tried to show Levi she was okay by smiling. It probably came off tense, so she added, "Nothing. Really. I thought I smelled some cheap cologne. It reminded me of Reggie, that's all."

Levi's face darkened to a deep maroon that made Rylie's nerves jitter. Levi had control of his awful temper now that he was older, of the bad anger genes their nonsainted father had given him. Special Forces and his work with the U.S. Marshals had taught him to manage the constant waves of rage that had driven their father to drinking and womanizing. Still, every now and then,

Rylie could see shadows of the demons Levi battled, and she couldn't help but wonder what would happen if he ever turned all that rage loose.

When Levi spoke again, his voice was low and grating. "Reggie Parker's still in Las Vegas."

Rylie's jitters shifted to surprise. She put a hand on her hip and stared into her brother's bluer than blue eyes. "You're keeping tabs on him? How? You don't work for the Marshals anymore."

"I have friends. They'll let me know if he's on the move—at least as soon as they know."

Rylie had no doubt Levi would be checking in with his buddies the instant he had a moment alone. Her big brother. He still had her back, no matter what. She approached him, tentative because he was glaring over her shoulder, studying the area behind her.

"It's probably nothing. Just a bad memory, or maybe Guerrero trying to give me the willies since I yelled at him on his own home turf."

Okay, that didn't help. Levi turned impossibly redder in the face. "You did what?"

"Did I forget to mention that?" Rylie heard the goofy nervousness in her own laugh and hated it. She'd never show this side of her to anybody but Levi. "I called him Francis. And accused him of being a crime lord, an asshole, and—oh, yeah—a *bad* crime lord since he claimed not to know what was happening to the trucks in Douglas."

For a few seconds, Levi tried to talk, but he just kept opening and closing his mouth. Then he just shook his head and stared at the cloudless sky. "There just aren't any words to describe you when you get on a roll."

"I can think of one. 'Bitch' would do nicely. Ask Guerrero. I'm sure he'd agree." Rylie patted her brother on the arm. "Come on. I only got half the boundary checked. Go with me to do the other half."

Levi walked straight to his horse and mounted, muttering, "Damn straight. I'm thinking I need to keep a much closer eye on you."

Clay tossed the manila folder onto his cluttered wooden desk and settled back in his chair. A frown creased his face as he stared out the glass window of his office and into the busy control room of the county sheriff's department.

He was having a hell of a time getting his mind on the job. He disliked the paperwork end of being sheriff, preferring fieldwork, so he delegated what office duties he could, but sometimes, there was nothing for it, especially when he had nothing but greenhorns and goof-offs in the office with him. The papers just had to be filled out.

Papers about truck thefts and interrupted truck thefts.

Thoughts of what he wanted to do with Rylie Thorn sure beat the heck out of signing dozens of documents or trying to catch a gang of thieves.

He remembered how she'd come storming into his office, her eyes blazing and how she'd laid into Deputy Quinn, then later, into Francisco Guerrero, as if the man couldn't snap his manicured fingers and have her throat slit on the spot. She'd looked so damn fiery and sexy that Clay had just stood and watched her carry on for at least a minute or two.

"Sheriff?" Quinn's voice cut into Clay's thoughts, forcing him back to the truck thefts at hand.

He glanced from his desktop to the dark-haired deputy who stood in the open doorway of his office. "Yeah?"

Quinn stepped into the room and hooked his thumbs in his front pockets. The armpits of his tan uniform were sweat-soaked, and perspiration coated the man's upper lip. "Another ranch got hit last night. They knocked out the man on guard and got three trucks."

"Damn." Clay slammed his hand on his desk and stood so abruptly he knocked his chair over, its thump like an exclamation point to his frustration. "This has been going on for two months. And that's two months too long."

"Uh-huh." Quinn's gaze dropped to the manila folder on Clay's desk. "What's your opinion on the Guerrero connection now that you've had a chance to think it over?"

Clay reached for the file and flipped it open. "Plenty likely, but no evidence against him or any of his known associates. Luke Denver, the MacKenna foreman, found some holes in his fence, his and Wade Larson's." Clay ran his finger down the page. "No vehicle tracks, no human tracks. Makes sense that they'd go out the way they came in and beat it for the border, especially if Guerrero was behind the operation, but since our contacts and informants are pretty sure they aren't crossing near here with the trucks . . . well, with Guerrero's auto dealerships, I suppose they could zip the vehicles straight to a local chop shop."

Stroking his hand over his mustache, Clay thought out loud,

"I can go talk to Guerrero again. Doubt I'll get anything fresh or new. This may not even be his game."

"What about Levi Thorn?"

Clay's gaze shot up to meet Quinn's blue eyes, which seemed unusually steady and focused. "What about him?"

Quinn shrugged. "Blalock and I have been looking into the desperate-for-cash possibilities, people in the area who are hard up for money. Levi's been short on funds for a while. The Thorn Ranch is in the red, so he has motive to earn a little money on the side. And he seems to have a bunch of money all of a sudden even though all those trucks just went missing from their spread. I hear he just about bought out Lowe's yesterday—ordered a huge bunch of lumber."

Frowning, Clay closed the manila folder. "Anything else?"

"A lady friend of mine works at the bank in Douglas." The deputy shifted and folded his arms across his chest. "She said Thorn got himself a safety deposit box, and he made a big deposit this morning. A good chunk of change. No way insurance paid off that fast on the stolen Thorn trucks."

With a sigh, Clay scrubbed his hand over his mustache. "Get a warrant for the box, but keep it quiet. See what you can dig up— but don't limit your investigation to him, not just yet. Everybody in this area's hurting. There's any number of people who could have gotten desperate enough to try to make a quick buck."

When the deputy left his office, Clay righted his chair and sank into it. If Rylie's brother ended up being a suspect, that sure put a damper on things. Hell, Rylie could be involved for all Clay knew—the Thorn Ranch was half hers, and he had an instinct she'd go to the mat and even die fighting before she let that property go down the drain.

But his gut told him otherwise, and unless his lust for her was screwing with his instinct, he was sure she was innocent. Levi Thorn, on the other hand, could very well be in the mess well past the crown of his Stetson.

The sound of a truck driving up to the ranch house jerked Rylie's heart into full gear. She dodged into her bedroom, chiding herself for being excited about a date. It had been years since she'd been nervous about going out, but there was something about Clay that made her body tingle just thinking about the man.

Rylie smoothed her short jean skirt as she checked her reflection in the mirror. She picked denim to commemorate what she was wearing when Clay first touched her, and she'd chosen a hot pink strapless top that bared her flat belly and slender shoulders.

She pushed her blond hair behind her ears and put a touch of gloss on her lips. A knock sounded at the door at the same time she spritzed on her vanilla musk cologne. After grabbing her jean jacket, she hurried to the door, only to see Levi walking in with Clay.

Her pulse skyrocketed at the sight of Clay, who was wearing a snug shirt that showed his cut physique to perfection and tight Wranglers that molded his muscular thighs—and that showed a promising bulge.

Levi frowned, took off his Stetson, and tossed it onto the hat rack, then ran his fingers through his blond hair. "You didn't tell me you had a date with the sheriff, Ry."

"Since when do I tell you about any of my dates?" She looked past Levi and smiled at Clay. "Hey there."

"Hey yourself." Clay touched the brim of his Stetson and smiled at Rylie.

"I'm gonna grab myself some eats." Levi nodded toward the kitchen, a tired, irritated look in his eyes. "Catch you later."

As Levi vanished into the kitchen, Clay murmured, "You look like spring come early."

She returned his smile with a sassy toss of her head, letting her gaze rake over him. Her voice was husky as she met his eyes. "I'd say you look like a real good reason to come . . . early."

A growl practically rumbled from his chest, and his green eyes darkened from crystal to almost jade. "Let's go."

Rylie slipped on her jacket and headed out the front door as Clay held it open for her. The cool night smelled clean and crisp, the sky clear with stars spattered across its expanse.

"You've got a choice to make," he said as they walked to the black truck parked out front.

She paused in front of the passenger door and looked up at him. "I told you, yes."

"This one's not a simple yes or no." He smiled and reached up to brush a strand of hair behind her ear. "I'd like to take you to dinner. The choice is, we can go to a nice place and hope for a quiet evening with no interruptions. Problem is, I can't seem to go out into public anymore without someone coming up and wanting to give me their opinion on one thing or another. You need to know that it's a real possibility."

Rylie leaned in toward him, enjoying his spicy male scent. "And choice number two?"

"Dinner at my place." His hand slid into her hair and he caressed her scalp. "Just the two of us."

"That's a no-brainer." She rose up on her toes and brushed her lips over his. "Let's go to your place."

Ten miles to his ranch. Clay wasn't sure he could do it. His hands and eyes wanted to wander straight to Rylie. The way her clothes hugged every curve, it nearly killed him. He'd been able to tell that she wasn't wearing a bra, and he'd almost bet that she didn't have on any panties, either. She had taken his dare. Damn, did he want to find that out for sure.

Instead of copping a feel, he kept his hands glued to the steering wheel as they'd talked about everything from the weather to what he'd done before he became sheriff. Whenever he tried to steer the conversation around to her, Rylie managed to evade his questions. As though she didn't like talking about herself . . . or maybe she had something to hide?

He pushed the thought to the back of his mind as he guided the truck from the highway, up the short dirt road, and then parked in front of his home.

"Nice," Rylie murmured, peering at the house through the starlit night. "What I can see of it, anyway."

Clay opened his door and walked around to help Rylie, only she was out of the truck before he made it to her side. He took her hand and led her to the house, enjoying the feel of her fingers twined with his.

He unlocked the front door and let her in, then closing it behind them. "How does steak sound?" he asked as he flipped on the track lighting.

"As long as it's medium rare, I'll love it."

"Done." He took off his Western hat and tossed it onto the back of a recliner, then raked his fingers through his hair.

Rylie slid off her jean jacket and laid it next to his hat as she glanced around the living room that was done in Western décor from oxblood-brown leather sofas and chairs to end tables made from knotty pine. Bookcases along one wall were filled with novels on the American West, along with tales by Zane Grey, Louis L'Amour, and other Western authors.

"For a bachelor, you have great taste." She moved to one end table and touched the bronze statue of a bucking bronco doing its best to unseat its rider.

Clay's mouth watered as he watched Rylie trail her fingers down the statue. He cleared his throat and came to stand beside her. "My youngest sister's into decorating and insisted that a sheriff needs appropriate digs."

"It suits you." Rylie tilted her head up and looked at him, her lips slightly parted, her chocolate eyes focused on him. "Rough . . . untamed . . . and utterly male." The desire in her gaze slammed into him like a fist to his gut. Before he even had a chance to act on his instinct, she moved into his arms and wrapped her arm around his neck.

"I don't know what you do to me," she murmured. "I barely know you, but all I can think about is sex when I'm near you."

"You make it real hard to think about anything else." Clay pulled her body tight against his and fisted his hands under her jean skirt. His fingers slid along her bare ass as he discovered she was wearing nothing underneath, just as he'd dared her to do. A groan rumbled from his chest, and he throbbed with scalding need to be buried inside Rylie's core.

She reached up and flicked her tongue over his bottom lip and then gently nipped it. Damn, but the sensation was erotic. He'd never had a woman bite his lip before, and he couldn't believe what it did to him.

Unable to stand her sweet torture any longer, Clay crushed his mouth against hers, devouring her, filling himself with her sweet taste. Rylie's tongue met his, her kiss as hard and demanding as his own.

He raised her skirt to her waist, then grabbed her ass, lifting her up and pressing her bare flesh against his erection. She wrapped her legs around his waist, clamping him tight as her hands clenched in his hair and they ravaged each other's mouth.

Rylie couldn't believe how wild she was for this man. She *needed* to feel his naked skin next to hers, to feel him sliding into her.

"I want you, Clay." Her voice was husky as she pulled back and looked into his eyes. "Now."

"Damn, Rylie." Clay moved his lips to her neck and she gasped at the sensual feel of his mustache along her throat. "I've never met a woman like you."

With her legs still wrapped around him, he walked to an over-stuffed chair near a fireplace. He set her down, her naked ass on the cool leather of the chair, her skirt hiked up to her waist. As he knelt between her thighs, she kicked off her shoes and spread her legs.

"I want you naked." Rylie reached for him, but he captured both her wrists in one of his big hands.

He gave her a sexy grin that sent tingles straight through her belly and made her absolutely wild for him. "I need a little appetizer first." With her wrists held in one of his hands, he pinned them over her head while pressing closer to her. His masculine scent filled her senses, driving her crazy, making her want him so badly that she wriggled and moaned.

With his free hand, Clay reached up and tugged on her strapless top, pulling it down to see her small breasts and pert nipples. "Mmmm. Beautiful," he murmured before lowering his head and licking one of her diamond-hard nubs.

Rylie gasped, her back arching up as feral sensations coursed through her body. She struggled to free her hands as Clay suckled first one nipple, then the other. His mustache brushed across her sensitized skin and she could swear she was going to come just from the sensation of his mouth, lips, and mustache on her breasts. The feel of her skirt and top around her waist, with the leather of the chair against her bared skin, was incredible.

"Let me touch you." She clamped her knees around his waist, locking her ankles behind his back and pressing his jean-clad crotch tighter to her sex.

"You enjoy watching people." He kissed a trail from her breasts to her neck as he spoke. "I'll bet you'd like to be tied up."

"God, yes." Rylie moaned at him, saying one of her fantasies aloud, and she knew she couldn't wait another moment to have him inside her.

"Such a wild little thing." Clay lowered her arms, but didn't release her wrists. Instead he kept a hold on them as he eased down. She smelled the scent of her juices as he widened her legs further and ran his tongue along the inside of her thighs.

"Dammit, Clay!" Rylie squirmed, dying for him to give her a little mercy. To do anything to bring her some relief. She'd never wanted anything as bad as she wanted Clay inside her.

"You like it fast and hard, don't you?" His tongue moved closer to where she wanted him to go. "Slow and easy drives you crazy, doesn't it?"

"Yes, you bastard." Rylie clenched her teeth and arched her back up off the chair. "Now quit making me wait."

Clay chuckled, the feel of his warm breath against her skin almost enough to send her over the pinnacle. "I was right that you shave." He ran his tongue up her smooth skin and she cried out from the feel of it. "And you're gorgeous."

Rylie was about to yell at him again when he pressed his mouth tight to her folds. He plunged his finger inside her, thrusting it in and out of her as he licked and sucked, driving her completely insane. She fought against his hold on her wrists, wanting to clench her hands in his hair, but at the same time totally turned-on by being held prisoner to his will.

Her climax hit her so hard that she shrieked and clamped her knees tight around his head. "Stop," she begged as aftershock upon aftershock wracked her body. "I can't take any more."

But Clay didn't stop, wouldn't stop, until she reached climax again. And then again.

Chapter 6

Rylie was still recovering from that third orgasm when Clay released her wrists, scooped her up, and stood. Her world spun and she gasped as she flung her arms around his neck and held on while he strode from the living room.

"Where are you taking me?" she asked as she clung to him.

"My room." His stride was deliberate, his jaw set as he carried her through the large home.

"'Bout time." She caught glimpses of a large stainless-steel kitchen that would make a chef envious, as well as a kitchen nook with a bay window and a formal dining room. The house smelled warm and inviting, a spicy masculine scent that reminded her of Clay.

His boots rang against the tile as he headed down a short hall and through double doors into a massive bedroom. Light from the hallway poured through the doors, illuminating the rough-hewn wooden furniture and a king-sized bed smack-dab in the middle of the room.

One-handed, he flipped on the lamp on the nightstand beside the bed, and the room filled with a soft amber glow. He set her on the comforter and tugged off her skirt and top before she had a chance to even think straight.

Rylie had never thought of herself as beautiful, not like her friend Skylar. As far as Rylie was concerned, she was too thin with not enough curves, as well as being small-chested. But right now, with the way Clay just stood there and looked at her with hunger, desire, and admiration in his green eyes, she felt absolutely gorgeous.

She eased off the comforter to stand on the small rug at his bedside as he toed off his boots and yanked off his socks. "Let me undress you," she said.

But when she reached for his shirt, he caught her wrists. "I don't know if I can wait that long."

"Fair's fair." Rylie gave him a saucy smile, but inside she was a quivering mass of lust. Every cell in her body screamed with need for this man. Need to have his naked form against hers, need to taste his skin, and need to see if he fit as perfectly inside as he did outside.

Clay released her, but a muscle in his cheek twitched and she could tell he was barely able to rein himself in. He clenched and unclenched his fists. "You'd better hurry, woman."

With a soft laugh, Rylie grabbed the bottom of his shirt, brought it up to his chest, and he helped her pull it over his head. The action mussed his thick sable hair, giving him an untamed and dangerous look.

"Mmmm." She ran her palms over his muscled chest, enjoying

the feel of him. "Now keep your hands to yourself while I get my turn at you." Breathing deeply of his scent, she leaned forward and flicked her tongue against his nipple, and delighted in the way he sucked in his breath. His biceps flexed as he fought for control.

His salty taste rolled over her tongue as she licked a path from one nipple, through the light dusting of hair on his chest, to the other nipple. Her hands continued exploring him, moving to his shoulders and along his arms to his wrists, and then back up and down his chest to his flat belly. She loved the ripple of muscle beneath his smooth skin and the way his taut stomach clenched beneath her touch.

"Rylie." A growl rumbled up in Clay's chest, reverberating through her as she continued kissing and licking him.

"Don't tell me you like it hard and fast." She trailed her tongue in lazy circles down his belly toward his waistband. "I thought you enjoyed slow and easy."

Clay thought he was going to climax in his jeans from the way the woman was torturing him. "Honey, when it comes to you, I have a feeling nothing's easy."

"Oh?" She tugged at his belt and pulled it out of the belt loops, her chocolate eyes meeting his. "I sure said yes mighty fast to you in the barn. What do you call that?" Rylie placed her hand on his cock and rubbed it through the denim.

He throbbed at her touch. "There's a difference between going after what you want and being easy."

"I like the way you think, cowboy." With nimble fingers she unfastened his jeans, tugged them down, and gasped when his erection sprang out. "Damn. I knew you were big, but . . . damn."

When she looked up at him, he raised an eyebrow at her wide-eyed expression.

A mischievous light sparked in her eyes. "In case you're wondering, that's a good thing."

He grinned as she pulled his jeans and briefs down past his hips and he stepped out of them. "Thank God for small favors."

Rylie knelt on the rug at his feet and wrapped her fingers around him. Her hair shimmered gold in the lamp's glow as she shook her head. "In your case, I'd say it was a rather large favor." Before he had a chance to respond, she swirled her tongue over his oh-so-sensitive head.

Clay's hips bucked and he slid his hands into her hair, unable to keep from touching her any longer. He could barely remember to breathe as he watched her lips slide down his shaft, taking him deep. Her mouth felt warm and wet, and better than he had imagined. And he had imagined plenty since meeting Rylie.

Her eyes met his as she continued easing her lips up and down. She moved one hand lower, toying with his sensitive sack while her other hand worked his staff in time with the motion of her mouth.

He clenched his fingers in her silken strands and gritted his teeth. "You're going to be swallowing real fast if you don't slow down."

In response she hummed, the vibration burning through him like a match-lit fuse. His groin tightened as the sensation shoved him over the edge and straight into an explosive orgasm.

Clay's hands clenched in Rylie's hair. She never let up, not for a moment. She would have kept going, but he managed to use his strength to his advantage and disengaged himself from her mouth.

His breathing came hard, sweat cooling his skin, as he braced his hands on her shoulders. Rylie grinned up at him, licking her lips like a cat cleaning the last bit of cream from her whiskers.

"Remind me not to piss you off," Clay murmured as he gripped her shoulders and drew her up to him. "You know how to get your revenge, don't you?"

Sliding her hands around his neck, she melded her lithe body against his. "Are you complaining?"

He chuckled and pressed his lips to her forehead. "Not on your life."

Satisfaction warmed Rylie's belly, knowing that she'd given him as much pleasure as he'd given her. A smile curved her lips as she nuzzled his chest. "You need time to regenerate, or are you ready?"

Clay growled as he grabbed her ass and pressed his thick erection to her belly. "What do you think?"

"Oooh, you're hard again." She stood up on her toes and brushed her mouth over his, loving the way his mustache felt against her lips. "So what are you waiting for?"

He clasped his big hands around her slim waist and practically tossed her onto the bed. Rylie laughed and brushed her hair out of her eyes. But her laughter faded as she saw the look on Clay's face—like he was up to no good.

His mustache twitched as he reached over to the dresser and grabbed something off the top, and Rylie caught the glint of metal.

She furrowed her brow as he moved onto the bed and knelt between her thighs. "What are you up to?" she asked as she tried to see what he was holding, but he held it behind his back.

Clay put his free hand by her head and captured her gaze with his. "So . . . you've fantasized about being tied up, have you?"

Warmth crept through Rylie, but it wasn't because she was embarrassed at having so easily admitted her fantasy. It was more the way he looked at her—like he intended to do something about it.

"Yeah . . ." No sooner had she said the word, than Clay brought the hand out that he'd been hiding and clamped cold steel around her wrist. "Hey—" she started, but he moved so fast that the next thing she knew he had her arms stretched over her head. He flipped the free cuff over the railing behind her, and then clasped the cuff to her other wrist.

"Oh, my God." Rylie twisted as she pulled against the cuffs, the metal slightly digging into her flesh. Her skin flooded with heat at the feel of being handcuffed and completely vulnerable to the man between her thighs. "I can't believe you really did it."

"Change your mind?" Clay pressed his cock to her belly, his gaze like green fire licking through her body.

"No way." Tingles skittered through Rylie's belly and her nipples tightened. "And in case you're wondering, I've had all my tests, I'm clean, *and* I'm on the pill. What about you, cowboy?"

"Clean bill of health all the way around." He gave her his sexy smile. "Shall I get out my donor card?"

"Anybody else, yes. You, I trust." She wrapped her legs around his waist. "So get on with it. Now."

His mouth came down on hers, crushing her lips, as if punishing her for making him desire her so much. Even though she knew it was fruitless, she pulled against the cuffs, wanting to reach around him and dig her nails into his back.

Clay hooked his arms under her knees and raised her up, opening her wide to him. He released one knee long enough to guide himself toward her slick opening. "Am I too big for you?"

"Never." She strained against the cuffs, arching her back. "Now, Clay!"

Rylie gasped as he slid his cock into her opening, stretching her with his thickness. He grabbed both of her ankles and moved them up to his neck, so that her feet were to either side of his head, and she could feel the softness of his hair along her instep. His eyes focused on hers, his breathing hard as he eased himself in another inch and then paused.

She raised her hips up, taking him deeper. "Give me all of you and stop messing with me."

The irritating man just grabbed her hips and gave her another fraction. "We have all night, honey."

Narrowing her eyes, Rylie did her best to glare at him. "There *will* be hell to pay later."

Clay grinned. "All right, little wildcat. You want it, then I'm gonna give it to you."

He thrust into her, burying himself. Rylie cried out at the sensation of having him so deep inside, stretching her and filling her completely.

"You okay?" Clay held still, sweat beading on his forehead and trickling down the side of his face.

"Oh, yeah." Rylie wiggled, enjoying the incredible fullness. "I'll be even better once you get to it."

With slow, even thrusts, he began moving within her core, holding her ass while he rose up on his knees. "You feel so good," he murmured.

She glanced down to where they were joined, mesmerized by the sight of him moving in and out of her. He was so big and thick, and it felt incredible. She had never been able to come from just penetration, but to her amazement, she already felt an orgasm coming on.

His pace increased, his flesh slapping against hers. "I love the way you watch me."

Her gaze moved to his and her stomach flipped at the look in his eyes. "Harder." Straining against the handcuffs, she tried to buck her hips. "I'm almost there."

Clay released her ass and reached around her legs to tweak her nipples, and at the same time began pounding into her like she wanted him to.

"Yeah . . . just like that." A faint buzzing started in Rylie's ears as he drove into her. The noise grew to a dull roar. Her stomach muscles clenched and her core contracted, gripping Clay tighter.

"Come on, honey." His voice was hoarse, like he could barely hold himself back from climaxing.

"Oh . . . my . . . *God*." Rylie's entire being vibrated as she grew closer and closer to the peak. "Don't stop, Clay. Harder. Harder!"

He growled as he pistoned his hips against hers.

"Yes!" she screamed as she came, her body jerking with the force of each wave of her orgasm.

Clay continued driving into her core, drawing along each undulation.

"Rylie. Oh, damn," he called out as he reached his climax. She felt every throb and pulse of his orgasm. He moved within her, slower and slower until he finally stopped, his hips fused against hers.

After a moment, he eased her legs down from around his neck so that her feet were resting on the comforter. His weight felt comfortable as he relaxed on top of her, his stubble-roughened cheek resting next to hers and his length still clenched deep in her depths. Smells of sex and sweat sifted through the air and Rylie sighed, more sated and content than she could remember feeling before.

"Mmmmm, Clay?" She moved her cheek against his, enjoying his stubble scraping her soft skin. "I hate to break this moment, but you think you could unlock these handcuffs?"

"I don't know." He propped himself up on both arms and his lips quirked in a grin. "Kinda like you right where I've got you."

"Oh?" Damn but he made her feel all quivery and gooey inside. "What do I have to do to convince you?"

Clay raised an eyebrow. "Of what?"

"That there'll be hell to pay if you don't get these things off me now."

With a soft laugh he rolled off of her, sliding out and leaving her empty without him. "Now supposing I can't find the key?"

Rylie glared at him. "Supposing I'm gonna kick your ass, cowboy."

Keys jangled as he returned. He held them in his palm, a wicked look in his green eyes. "How about we strike a deal?"

"Clay . . ." She swallowed back her retort as his gaze swept over her naked form from her arms stretched over her head, on down, settling on her shaved sex. While he studied her his cock lengthened, and her mouth watered to taste him again. He looked magnificent, his body so muscular and sculpted. Rylie's nipples hardened and her core flooded as he smiled and met her eyes.

He sat on the edge of the bed, and brushed his lips over hers. "I'll let you go if you promise to stay the night."

Rylie's breath caught, and she went still, pulling against the handcuffs. Her heart pounded out a strange cadence in her throat. "I don't stay the night with anyone."

"Why?"

She didn't think she could answer, but heat—not a good kind—drove her words. "It's one thing to enjoy sex. It's another to wake up with a man and have breakfast with him. I don't know you like that, cowboy."

I don't know anybody like that, and I'm not sure I want to.

"Stay with me." His words were a demand, definitely not a request.

She shook her head, but when she spoke, the word barely came out in a whisper. "No."

"That's my condition, little wildcat." Clay pressed his forehead to hers. "I aim to tame you."

Chapter 7

The man was serious—Rylie could see it in Clay's eyes, could hear it in his tone. Yet at the same time she couldn't believe he intended to keep her cuffed to the bed until she agreed to spend the night with him.

It took her a few seconds to beat down the instinctive panic and rage. She might be trapped by his damned cuffs, but she would not let him or anyone force her to be intimate in ways she'd rather avoid.

Look at him. He's not trying to trap you. He's trying to tease you. To please you. Don't hold him accountable for your screwed-up childhood.

She felt herself relaxing. Something about Clay made that easier.

"What'll it be, honey?" Clay brushed his lips over hers, and sparks skittered through her belly like a dozen firecrackers. "I'll feed you in bed if you'd rather be cuffed all night."

All right. *Fine.* If he wanted to play rough, she'd give him as good as he dished out.

Like hell he would tame her. And before sunrise she *would* get her own revenge.

When he drew back, Rylie glared at him the best she could manage. "I'll spend the night, but only because I don't particularly feel like being cuffed to the bed."

A smug smile crossed Clay's handsome features as he reached up, removed the cuffs, and tossed them on the comforter. He massaged her wrists, the sensation of his touch soothing and arousing all at once. Passion burned through Rylie, coupled with warmth from the caring she witnessed in his expression.

Even though she barely knew him, somehow this man stirred emotions and longings within her that she didn't want to admit, and had never allowed herself to consider.

Like a possibility of happiness and a future with one man.

No. Make-believe and fairy tales: she didn't believe in either. A father who wouldn't work and liked to scream at his wife and kids, and a mother who couldn't stand up to him had taught her way too much about what happens to people who believe in magic.

Clay pressed his lips to the inside of one of her wrists, and flicked his tongue against her pulse point, sending a shiver throughout her body. "You ready for some chow?" he murmured.

"S-sure." She frowned at the way her voice trembled. What the hell was he doing to her?

Satisfaction curled in Clay's gut as he took her by the hand and helped her off the bed. He'd always been able to trust his instinct, and that instinct had told him from the beginning that Rylie shied away from real intimacy. Why she was afraid of a serious relationship, he didn't know, but he was determined to find out.

And by the time all was said and done, she'd be his.

Rylie took her hand from his grasp and scooped his shirt from the floor. Her voice was muffled as she pulled it over her head. "So what's for dinner, other than steak?"

When she reappeared, static caused her hair to poke up all over her head in a blond halo. She was so petite that his shirt reached her knees, and she looked like a woodland pixie. Clay grinned, holding back a laugh.

"What?" Rylie put her hands on her slim hips and narrowed her gaze.

"You." Shaking his head, he took her by the shoulders and kissed her forehead, then drew back to look at her again. "You're adorable."

"Hmph." She tried to look grouchy, but in his gut Clay knew it was all an act. For some reason she preferred to keep an emotional distance, which was something he'd have to change.

He released her shoulders to grab his briefs and jeans off the floor, then pulled them on. "How about rolls, tossed salad, and mashed potatoes? I might even be able to come up with something for dessert, too."

"I have to warn you, I'm not into cooking, so I won't be much help." Rylie walked by his side as he headed out of the bedroom toward the kitchen. "If it wasn't for prepackaged meals and the microwave, Levi and I would probably starve."

At the mention of her brother, a cloud passed through Clay's consciousness. It probably wasn't real smart of him to get busy with a suspect's sister, but when it came to Rylie, Clay had to make an exception.

"Dinner's my treat, so sit your pretty ass down," he said as they reached the kitchen. He took a package of T-bones out of the fridge and brought them to the grill built into the center of the stovetop. "My mom saw to it that my sisters and I learned how to cook."

"Ooooh, a man who's great in bed *and* knows how to whip up a meal." Rylie moved to the breakfast bar and eased up onto a stool. "If you clean, too, I think I've struck pay dirt."

Clay grinned as he turned on the grill, then grabbed a stone-ware plate out of the cabinet. "I have a housekeeper who comes in a couple of times a week."

"Even better." Mischief sparked in Rylie's eyes. "Leaves more time for all that great sex."

His gaze met hers. "Better watch it, honey, or dinner'll be late."

"Promises, promises." Her voice was teasing, but her nipples poked through his shirt. He had no doubt she'd love it if he took her right there in the kitchen.

She cleared her throat. "So . . . you actually like to cook?"

With effort, Clay reined in his lust and took the steaks out of the package. "I have nothing against going out for a meal or heating up something in the microwave." He slapped the steaks onto the stoneware plate and seasoned them liberally with salt and pepper. "But sometimes I find it kinda relaxing to cook up a good meal, like Mom makes."

Rylie enjoyed watching Clay as he fixed their dinner. The man was powerful and sensual, in command of his environment no matter where he was. Even in the kitchen.

He looked so damn sexy in only his jeans, his chest bare and hair mussed. Her palms itched to touch him again, and she couldn't wait to breathe deep of his masculine scent.

For a while she was silent as she studied him, his muscles rippling in the soft lighting. With efficient movements he cut up potatoes and placed them in a pot with water to boil, then started putting together a salad with fixings he grabbed from the fridge.

Cocking her head to the side, she asked, "I've been wondering what you were doing on my ranch that night we, ah, met."

The corner of his mouth quirked into a smile as he chopped a tomato on a cutting board. "When you were being a Peeping Tomasina?"

"Peeping Tomasina, huh?" A giggle escaped her before she could stop it. "Don't tell me you were being Tom."

"Not intentionally." He tossed the tomatoes into a bowl with lettuce greens. "I was coming out to take your theft report myself, and to warn you off pulling any more stunts with Guerrero. I wanted to see you again, so I told the deputies I'd do it, then I got hung up with some emergencies and it got late."

"Ah." Rylie propped her elbow on the breakfast bar as she watched him, her chin resting in her hand. "You wanted to see me again. I think I like that." She gazed at him, wanting more than that, more of him. "So, tell me about your family. Like how many sisters you have."

"Three." Clay gave her a quick grin as he tossed the steaks onto the grill. "I'm the oldest. I think that's what got me interested in law enforcement—I was always on the lookout for those girls. They were bound and determined to get into as much trouble as possible, and I was determined to keep them out of it."

"Uh-huh. An overprotective older brother." Rylie smiled at the thought of Clay chasing off his sisters' boyfriends. "I have one of those. Levi made it known that if any guys messed with me, he'd kick their asses." She shook her head and rolled her eyes. "Needless to say, it was not real good for my social life, considering Levi was one of the buffest jocks in school." Of course he'd saved her ass once, too, and they had survived the collective hell that had been their warring parents together.

Was it her imagination, or did Clay's eyes narrow at the mention of her brother's name?

But Clay just nodded and gave her a quick grin. "I bet he had to kick a lot of ass to keep the guys away from you."

"Yeah, right." Rylie snorted. "I didn't develop as fast as most girls, so I was more like one of the guys. At least until I was a junior and my boobs actually decided to grow, even if it was just a little bit."

Clay's eyes shot from the steaks to Rylie. "You're perfect." He set down the fork he'd been holding, and in just a couple of steps, he was at her side. She caught her breath as he lifted the shirt she was wearing and captured her breasts in his hands. "Pert, beautiful nipples. And more than a mouthful."

He ducked his head and suckled one of her hard nubs. Rylie gasped as he flicked his tongue over her nipple, then gently pulled at it with his teeth, before moving to the other breast. In the background, she could hear the sizzle of the steaks on the grill and the hiss of water on the stovetop as the potatoes boiled over. But Clay didn't seem to care. His thumb found her sweet spot and he thrust his fingers into her core.

Rylie slid her hands into his hair and held on, lost in the feelings he stirred within her. A moan escaped her lips as he sucked and gently bit at each nipple while his thumb teased her, his fingers still deep in her depths.

The orgasm flamed through her body, and she cried out from the searing pleasure of her release. Her hips jerked against Clay's hand as he continued to move his fingers in and out.

"Stop." She put her hands on his shoulders, her body throbbing. "No more."

Clay eased his fingers from her core and raised his head. His eyes fixed on her and he licked his fingers. Every slow stroke of his tongue was like he was touching her, tasting her. She couldn't stop trembling from her climax.

"Damn, you taste good." He brushed his mouth over hers, his mustache tickling her lips, the warmth of his breath adding heat to her blood. "I'd better see to dinner before something burns," he murmured, then turned back to the stove.

Too late, the thought went through Rylie's fuzzy mind. She was burning all over.

After they'd eaten a bowl of chocolate fudge ice cream for dessert, Clay took Rylie on a tour of his ranch-style home. He enjoyed showing it to her, and how she seemed to appreciate the custom-built house. He'd had it built only a year prior, and it was his sanctuary away from the demands of his job and the political aspects of being the county sheriff.

They ended up in his den, where he worked at home from time to time. He flicked on the track lighting, which illuminated glossy oak furnishings and floor-to-ceiling shelves lining two walls. Books on Arizona, Native American, U.S., and world history lined the shelves, along with professional journals and handbooks, biographies, and anything else that had caught his interest.

Navajo artwork that he'd collected over the years covered the walls as well as dotting the shelves, along with pictures of his family. The room smelled of books, lemon oil polish, and of the case of cherry pipe tobacco that he kept to remind him of his dad.

From off the oak credenza, Rylie picked up a carved wooden caricature of an old cowboy with a drooping mustache and a ten-gallon hat that looked like it had a hole shot through the top of the crown. "This is great. Who's the artist?"

"I am." Clay smiled when her gaze cut to his, her eyes wide. "Wood carving is a hobby of mine. I have a little workshop in the back of the house."

Wrinkling her nose, she placed the cowboy back on the shelf. "That's disgusting."

He raised a brow. "You don't like it?"

"Love it." Rylie poked his chest with one finger. "What's disgusting is that you're not only fantastic in bed, know how to cook, have great taste in decorating, and are well read, but you're artistic, too."

His mouth curved into a grin. "Don't forget kind to animals and small children."

"So I see." She walked away from him to the shelves and ran her fingers along one of the framed photographs. "Whose kids?"

"Between two of my three sisters, I have six nieces and nephews. That's Brian, the youngest of the bunch. They're good kids."

Clay eased behind Rylie, gripped her shoulders and nuzzled her neck. "Do you want to have rug rats of your own one day?"

A tingling sensation sparked in her belly, but she refused to dwell on it. Instead she shrugged and moved her hand away from the picture. "I don't plan on ever getting married, so likely not."

Clay turned her around and moved her so that her butt was backed up to the massive oak desk. "What's spooked you?" He hooked his forefinger under her chin and raised it so that her eyes met his. "Why are you afraid of getting serious about anyone?"

"Because relationships never last." Rylie's gaze was defiant, but her hand went to her earlobe and she tugged on the gold earring. "And the ones that do, most of those go to shit. I wouldn't put any kid through what I grew up with."

With a gentle hand, he swept a strand of blond hair from her face. "And what's that?"

"Being torn between parents who hate each other while they play tug-of-war with you." Her jaw hardened and she pulled harder at her ear. "Having your mom play doormat for years, then take off with some man, and never seeing her again because she'd rather run away and play than be around her own kids. Watching your dad marry and divorce so many times you can't remember the names of all your stepparents or stepbrothers and sisters. All I ever heard was yelling and fighting, Clay. That's what I know about real relationships."

He brushed his knuckles along her cheek to her ear and captured her hand in his, pulling it away from her lobe. "Honey, just because your parents didn't know how to make a relationship work doesn't mean you'll follow in their footsteps." Clay released her to let his hands slide down to her waist, then drew her closer. "You're not them."

Rylie could hardly think with him pressed against her belly. Now was not the time to think about her history, or her future. She wanted him again, and she wanted him *now*. Bracing her hands on the desk behind her, she widened her stance. "Shut up and get inside me."

Clay's green eyes flared. In a quick movement that left her breathless, he raised her up and placed her on the desk, its polished surface cool beneath her bare ass. He yanked the shirt over her head and tossed it on the floor, then unfastened his jeans and shoved them with his briefs down his hips.

She spread her thighs and he guided himself into her depths in one quick thrust. Pure pleasure rippled through Rylie at the feel of him inside her, and she wrapped her legs around his waist. She flattened her hands on the desktop and tilted her head back, lost in the sensations.

"Watch." Clay's voice was gruff as he grasped her thighs with his hands. "Watch me take you."

Rylie looked down at where they were joined. The mere sight of him thrusting in and out was enough to drive her closer and closer to peak.

Lowering his head, he pressed his mouth against hers, urging her up to meet him. His tongue slid between her lips, matching the motion and rhythm of his movements.

She moaned into his mouth, dizzy, wild with lust. The smell of their sex was an aphrodisiac, heightening her arousal, sending her senses spiraling. Her body was hot, her nipples tingling with every brush of his solid chest.

He raised his head and glanced to where they were joined, then back to her eyes. "You fit me perfectly, Rylie Thorn." He drove into her, harder and harder yet.

She gasped and her eyes widened as her body trembled with the oncoming climax

"That's it." Clay gripped her legs tighter, never slowing in his motion. "Come on, honey."

Rylie cried out as the muscles in her belly contracted with each wave of her orgasm. Every thrust sent another swell of pleasure throughout her body. It seemed like her climax would never end. Like she'd be locked with him forever, her body shuddering with every crest and ebb.

Even as he shouted her name, even as he jerked and throbbed within her core, Rylie was swept away in a tidal wave of sensation that threatened to drown her.

Threatened to steal her heart and never let go.

The telephone's incessant ring broke into Clay's climax-fogged mind. If it didn't mean pulling out from Rylie's warm depths, he would have reached over and thrown that damn telephone out the window.

"You're in hot demand, Sheriff." Rylie's teasing voice murmured in his ear as the answering machine clicked on and she heard a standard message being played. "You gonna get that?"

"No." The word was a rumble in Clay's chest as he kissed the soft skin of her neck. "Whoever it is can go to hell for all I care."

The outgoing message stopped, and then Deputy Quinn came on the line. "Sheriff, I need a word with you. It's about—"

The moment he heard Quinn's voice, Clay moved so fast that he was able to pick up the phone just as the man said, "Levi Thorn."

"I'm right here," Clay growled, yanking up his jeans and looking away from Rylie's frown. "What's so damn important that you had to call me at home on my night off?"

"Uh, well . . ." The deputy sounded like he was uncomfortable with the news he was relaying. "Wade Larson said he was out checking his fence line the other night. The same night someone tried to steal trucks from the MacKenna's. Claims he saw a horse and rider leaving the Flying M Ranch—and he recognized the horse."

Clay's gaze flicked to Rylie. She was still naked, but now looking at the carvings of old cowpokes that he'd done. "And?" he prompted Quinn.

"Larson says it was Rylie Thorn's Appaloosa and the rider was the same size as Levi. Larson wasn't sure, but he thought Levi was following a group of men who were running from the scene. Could have been chasing them instead of getting out of Dodge—but then, why wouldn't he have told us that?"

"Shit." Clay drew in a harsh breath and Rylie's gaze shot to him. She bit her lower lip and scooped the T-shirt off the floor and left his den, probably to give him some privacy.

"What do you want me to do, Sheriff?" Quinn asked in an even tone.

"Nothing yet. Let me check a few things out." Clay stared at the door Rylie had disappeared through. "You just see what else you can dig up. And I still don't want you to narrow the focus. Got me?"

After he hung up with Quinn, Clay stroked his hand over his mustache, trying to puzzle through what was going on. Levi Thorn had motive and opportunity, but did he have the connections to swipe trucks, make it seem like one of Guerrero's gang rackets, then liquidate the trucks for cash?

Could Levi be desperate enough to be working with Guerrero? *A big brother trying to save the ranch and look after his little sister . . .*

Although the evidence was starting to point to Thorn, something in Clay's gut told him it was all too neat. There was a hell of a lot going on around here. More than what met the eye.

He picked up the receiver and dialed up Rocky Brogan, a buddy of his that could do some quick, efficient research—beyond anything he could manage to scrape together through the sheriff's department.

"Brogan here." The man's baritone came on the line.

"Clay Wayland." His eyes remained on the doorway, making sure Rylie didn't come marching through, and he kept his voice low. "I need you to get some down and dirty on a few of characters, and I need it completely off the radar."

"Shoot, pardner."

"All currently reside in or around Douglas, Arizona." Clearing his throat, Clay continued, "Zack Hunter: ICE agent, recently married to a local ranger, Skyler MacKenna. He's from these parts, but stayed away a long time."

Clay waited until Brogan gave him the go-ahead. "Wade Larson, general malcontent, owner of the Coyote Pass Ranch." He hesitated, then tacked on, "And Levi Thorn, part owner of the Thorn Ranch. And see if your sources drag up anything about new Guerrero activity in this area. I'm particularly interested in stolen vehicles."

Brogan repeated all the information and punctuated it with a small grunt. "Give me a couple of days."

"Thanks," Clay replied. "I'll look for it Monday."

After he placed the receiver back on the cradle, Clay rubbed his forehead, trying to ease the beginnings of a headache. Damn, but he didn't like the way things were turning. Didn't like it at all.

Chapter 8

Golden light of a new morning spilled through the shutters and onto Clay's eyelids, but he was too comfortable holding his little wildcat. He kept his eyes closed, enjoying the feel of her in his arms, filling his lungs with her perfume of vanilla musk and the scents of their mingled sex.

Rylie stirred next to him, her hip rubbing against his hard-as-iron length. "Better watch it," he murmured, his voice thick with sleep. "Or I might just have to wake you properly."

"Oh, yeah?" Her tone was light and teasing as she caressed his forearm.

But then he heard a familiar metal click at the same moment cool metal clamped around his wrist.

His eyes shot open and he yanked his arm, only to have metal dig into his flesh. He was handcuffed to the bed rail.

Rylie giggled, rolling away from him and off the bed before he had the chance to grab her with his free hand. She dragged the comforter along with her so that he was completely naked, then dropped it to the floor as she said, "I told you that you'd pay."

"You sure did." Clay couldn't help but grin at the sight of her eyes glinting with laughter. But his smile faded as his gaze traveled down her length, from her tousled hair to her pert nipples, on past her flat stomach and below.

He was so hard he was afraid he wouldn't last but a few seconds. "Over here. Now."

Her grin widened. "Don't you know? Paybacks are a bitch, sugar."

Letting her gaze linger on him, she licked her lips. Something told Clay he just might enjoy her version of paybacks. But then again, when it came to Rylie Thorn, nothing was a certainty. And nothing was easy.

"I have to teach you a lesson." She walked around the bed, studying him like a buyer examining a bull at an auction. "Now, I could just leave you locked up . . . Take your truck and go on home."

Clay frowned. "Uh, honey—"

"Hold on, I'm thinking here." Rylie held up her hand, a look of serious consideration on her face. "Or, I could force you to have wild sex with me."

"That'd be a hardship." Clay's cock jumped against his belly, and he held back a grin. "But I think I could manage."

"Hmmm." She strolled closer to his side of the bed, but kept her enticing body out of reach. "Of course, I could always get my revenge in another way."

A rumble of sheer lust rose up in his throat, and he bit the inside of his cheek so hard he tasted blood.

"Do you want to touch me, Clay?" Slowly, deliberately, she ran her tongue along her lower lip while she cupped her breasts in her palms, her chocolate eyes focused on him.

"Yeah." His voice was hoarse and he swallowed, hard, then swallowed again as she pulled at her nipples. Nipples he wanted to suck, and lick, and nip at with his teeth.

A sensual smile teased the corner of her mouth as she let one of her hands drift down her flat belly to her silken sex. "Would you like to see me touch myself?"

"Rylie . . ." Clay groaned and pulled against the restraint, wondering if he could bust the rail, snatch her before she knew he was loose, and take her ten ways till Sunday. He was so hard his erection practically pointed toward the ceiling.

"How about if I make myself come while you watch?" She widened her stance and slipped her fingers lower. Her lips parted and her eyelids fluttered as she stroked herself with one hand while tweaking her nipple with her other. "I like how you feel inside me, Clay." Again she licked her lips, this time her gaze focused on his erection. "Would you like to be inside me now?"

"Hell, yes." The cuff rattled against the rail as he strained against it.

"What if I sit on your face?" Rylie seemed lost in the sensations of taunting him while stroking herself. "Would you like that?"

He clenched his fist and practically growled at her. "Why don't I show you?"

She turned her back to him and bent over, her legs parted so that he could clearly see her beautiful shaved skin, and her fingers teasing, teasing, teasing. Looking over her shoulder, she said, "Would you like to take me from behind?"

Clay roared and slid his legs over the side of the bed, trying to grab her with his free hand. The cuffs slid along the rail and held fast, keeping Clay only inches from reaching Rylie.

She taunted him as she looked over her shoulder and gave him that sexy smile. "Yeah, that's it."

He yanked so hard against the restraints that the bed moved a good six inches.

Rylie gasped as Clay hooked his free arm around her waist and pulled her ass tight against him. "You need to be punished, woman."

"I *have* been a bad girl." She bent even lower, rubbing her ass against him. "So what are you going to do about it?"

"Ride you until you can't walk straight." Clay stepped back against the bed, dragging Rylie with him. In a quick motion, he flipped her around. She squealed as she found herself sprawled on the bed, her ass sticking up in the air. It was a tricky maneuver, considering he was handcuffed to the rail, and it didn't leave a lot of room for error. But he was a man on a mission.

He guided himself into her wet folds, nudging her legs farther apart. The walls of her core gripped him tight and he damn nearly came.

She moaned as he sank deep inside her. Gripping the bedsheet in her hands, she pressed her ass back against him. "I've been a *real* bad girl. I think you'd better take that into consideration."

The cuff yanked against Clay's wrist as he powered himself within Rylie's slick depths. Her passionate cries added even more fuel to his frenzied thrusts.

He didn't have much more time before he came. This woman drove him crazy, made him so damn hot with lust he couldn't think straight. As he pumped in and out of her, he reached around her hips and stroked her swollen center.

That was all it took. She screamed into the bedsheet, her body tensing against him, the muscles of her core clenching him tight. Clay bit back a shout as he came. He throbbed and pulsed as he collapsed against her backside, doing his best to keep his weight off her.

"Mmmm." Rylie sighed, enjoying the feel of Clay's muscled body pressed along her length. She wiggled her hips and was rewarded by the feel of him hardening inside her. "What's for breakfast?"

Clay chuckled and pressed his lips to her hair. "Depends on whether or not you unlock this cuff."

"And if I say no?"

"Then I keep you right here where I've got you."

"That's not so bad." She shimmied her hips again. "I kinda like it."

"Uh-huh." The cuff rattled against the bed rail as he shifted. "I'm getting a cramp here."

"Ahhh, poor baby." Rylie tried to move out from under Clay's weight, but he had her pinned tight to the mattress. "Okay. Let me go and I'll get the key."

"How do I know I can trust you?" Clay withdrew from her core and eased his weight to the side, but still kept his free arm around her waist. "After all, you are a real bad girl."

"Well, next time you can spank me." Her remark was flippant, but in the next second Clay smacked her ass with the flat of his hand. "Ow!" Surprise shot through Rylie. His hand was so large compared to her butt that both cheeks stung, yet the sensation made her ache.

"If you're bad, that's what you can expect." He nuzzled her nape, his breath warm across her shoulder blades.

Rylie moaned. "Don't forget. This bad girl always gets her revenge."

"I'm counting on it, little wildcat." Low laughter rumbled through Clay's chest. "I'm counting on it."

Clay asked Rylie to spend all of Sunday with him, but she insisted she had to get home and take care of her share of chores around the ranch. He had a feeling, though, that it had more to do with her fear of getting too close to him. Even after all that they had shared since last night, he could sense her pulling away from him, trying to distance her emotions and her heart.

After a leisurely breakfast, Clay drove Rylie back to her ranch, and then walked her up to the front porch. She paused, her fingers gripping the handle of the screen door, and raised her eyes to meet his. "Thanks for the hot time, cowboy." Her tone was light, but her eyes were so dark they were almost black. Like she wanted him right this minute.

He reached up and caught a wisp of her blond hair, fingering the soft strands. "How 'bout I take you out for dinner tomorrow night. I know a great Mexican restaurant."

She shivered, as though unnerved by his nearness. "I thought you were worried about being mobbed in public."

"It's not so bad early in the week." He moved in closer, pressing her up against the screen. "It's easier to tell a few people to go to hell, rather than a large crowd."

"I . . . I'm busy Monday." Rylie swallowed, her throat working. She put her palms against Clay's chest, as if she was trying to bolster her determination. "Actually, the whole week's pretty tight."

"Sure it is." He brushed his lips across her forehead. Even though they'd taken a shower together, he thought he could still smell the scent of their sex. "Change your plans."

"Can't." Her response was barely a whisper as his mouth trailed from her forehead to her ear. She clenched her hands in his shirt and tilted her head back, a soft moan rising in her throat.

"My dad always taught me there's no such word as 'can't.'" Clay moved his lips over hers. "Anything you truly want, you can have. Anything you put your mind to, you can do."

"And you put your mind to taking me out?" Her breath was warm against his mouth, her gaze focused on his lips.

"Uh-huh." Clay took possession of Rylie's mouth, his hands sliding around her slender waist and drawing her tight along his length. The woman was fire in his blood, singeing him, until she'd burned a permanent hole in his heart. No way was she getting away from him, no matter what she might think.

Her fingers gripped his shirt tighter as their mouths mated. His tongue gained entrance to her willing mouth, and her sweet taste swept through him like the warm rush of rain in a summer thunderstorm.

"Where the hell have you been?" A man's voice growled from the other side of the screen door.

The sound of her brother's voice startled Rylie. She jerked her head back, breaking the kiss, but Clay held on to her, keeping her pinned to him.

"Dammit, don't sneak up on me like that, Levi." Her tone was slightly breathless as she turned to look at her brother through the screen door.

She glanced back up at Clay and saw a predatory look in his eyes. " 'Morning, Thorn," Clay said as he pulled her away from the door, giving Levi enough room to open it and step through.

Levi glared at Clay, that protective-older-brother look in his blue eyes, then turned his frown on Rylie. "Since when do you stay out all night without calling home?"

"You knew where I was." Rylie straightened to her full five feet four inches, and raised her chin. "I'm twenty-eight years old. I certainly don't need to report in to you."

"Well, how about a bit of common courtesy?" He brushed past her and Clay, and headed to the far end of the porch where an enormous box stood that she hadn't noticed before. "You had me worried."

"You could have called." She pushed away from Clay, and felt relieved when he let her go. "What's that?"

Levi dug in his front pocket and pulled out his pocketknife. "New water heater."

"We can't afford a new heater." Rylie put her hands on her hips and frowned at her brother. "How in the hell did you pay for it?"

He shrugged and used his knife to slice the plastic straps around the cardboard. "Don't worry. It's taken care of."

"What do you mean, don't worry?" If there was one thing Rylie couldn't stand, it was to be told to butt out of something she considered to be her business.

"I said, don't worry about it." Levi spoke through clenched teeth and gave her "the look" that said they'd discuss it when they didn't have company.

Her gaze shot to Clay. He had his thumbs hooked through his belt loops and was watching Levi cut open the box. "Need some help getting that inside the house?" Clay asked.

"Sure." Levi gave a quick nod. "If you have the time."

"I've got all day." Clay winked at Rylie. "I can help you install it, if you'd like. I've got some experience there."

Rylie raised her hands in exasperation. Here she thought she'd be escaping his incredible masculine magnetism, at least for the rest of the day. Sure, the sex was great, but she needed time to gather her wits. Needed space away from this man who turned her inside out and made her feel like a simpering little fool.

"All right." She moved to the screen door and propped it open. "You two *men* enjoy tearing up the place. Just don't expect me to serve anything fancier than a pitcher of iced tea and a box of macaroni and cheese."

Clay flashed her a quick grin. "I like mine extra, extra cheesy."

"I'd like lemon but no sugar in my tea, Ry," Levi called out as he ripped the cardboard away from the new water heater.

Shaking her head, Rylie headed into the house and let the screen door slam behind her.

Men.

* * *

Clay worked with Levi in companionable silence for a while, debating various ways to ask him a few casual questions without putting him on the defensive. In the end, it was Levi who broke the ice after spending ten minutes cussing a pipe fitting without ever saying the same word twice.

He pulled up, wiped sweat off his face with his glove, and tossed Clay a half-sheepish glance. "Sorry. My temper gets away from me sometimes. I got it from my father."

Clay sat down on the floor outside the closet where the water heater was trying to refuse to fit. "Rylie's mentioned a little about that guy. Sounds like a real prince."

"Dad was a shit, but I know he tried to love us." The focus in Levi's blue eyes sharpened, and Clay thought he caught a trace of U.S. Marshal in the man, the natural sureness of a hunter who could stalk and kill bad-ass villains without much remorse. "How about you, Wayland? You got a temper?"

And just like that, I'm the one being interrogated. Clay knew the man wasn't posturing, but he was definitely making an implied threat. Or, more like a promise. It didn't rattle or offend Clay in the least. He appreciated the fact that Rylie's brother looked after her. "I've got a little bit of a temper, but my job requires me to keep a cool head."

Not good enough. Clay could tell by the frown stamped on Levi's serious features. "Would you ever turn that temper on my sister?"

"Never."

That, Clay saw, was good enough. The frown eased into a more relaxed expression as Levi heard the truth in Clay's voice. He stepped out of the closet and sat on the floor across from Clay, and for a few seconds, they gulped iced tea in silence.

"Ry's tough as nails," Levi said, looking directly into Clay's face, "but she's soft, too. I take it personal when somebody steps on her."

"Won't happen. Not with me." Clay put his tea down, his muscles tightening as instinct told him Levi might be on the verge of saying something more important than the whole big-brother routine.

Levi let out a long breath, then stared up at the ceiling. "She told me about getting in Francisco Guerrero's face. I think she may have stepped in it with that asshole."

Clay felt his tension slowly converting to anger and wariness. "What makes you say that?"

"He sent some boys around to rattle her . . . more than once, I think. I headed them off the last time, even went and had a word with Guerrero." Levi's blue eyes drilled into Clay. "I'm not sure he listened, if you get my drift. Maybe he'd listen to you a little harder, since you've got a badge and a gun to back it up."

The anger in Clay's gut grew until he knew his face had to be turning red. He picked up his tea again, clenching his fist around the glass and fighting an urge to plow out of there and pound on Guerrero until the sneaky little shit couldn't bother anyone ever again. "No problem. I'll make sure your message gets through."

Levi nodded, and Clay felt the common ground between them getting firm.

"If he comes after Rylie, I'll take him down." Levi's expression was earnest and intense. "You can do whatever you have to do to me after that—I'm just letting you know, man to man."

Clay put down his tea and stood, and Levi got to his feet and faced him. Clay put out his hand to the other man, and made sure to keep his gaze steady. "If he comes after Rylie, I'll be standing right next to you, Levi."

Levi hesitated for a second, then shook his hand. "Okay, then. And thanks."

Clay wanted to tell the guy not to thank him, not yet, but he didn't want to destroy the small amount of trust they had just built unless he absolutely had to. He liked Levi, both as Rylie's brother and as a potential friend. Maybe even as a deputy if he could talk the man into living for law enforcement again.

I sure as shit don't want to arrest him.

Chapter 9

Guerrero wasn't at Arizona Motors South when Clay went looking. He had to track the bastard down at Arizona Motors West, the lower-rent operation. AM-West was nothing but a trailer on a lot, with old paneling, ugly orange carpeting, and a loud rattling air conditioner that fogged up the front windows.

Guerrero had a few thugs lurking around the lot, but they didn't do anything but nod at Clay as he closed the front door of the trailer behind him—and locked it. He saw Guerrero at a desk to his left, and when Guerrero stood, Clay saw that he was wearing jeans and a white T-shirt, perfect for the neighborhood.

So Armani's his theme only when he's dealing with an Armani crowd. He's a chameleon. He'll be whoever he has to be to get the job done.

Guerrero came out from behind his desk and shook Clay's hand, and Clay forced himself not to break the man's fingers with his grip.

He didn't even let Guerrero sit back down before he got straight to it.

He let go of Guerrero's hand and glared straight at him. "You sent men to the Thorn Ranch."

Guerrero's eyebrows shot up and his jaw loosened, but when he spoke, he sounded like every word was rehearsed. "I did. I wanted to see if she needed assistance around the ranch, since she wouldn't allow me to help her with a rental truck."

"Bullshit." Clay got a little closer to him and caught a whiff of strong, expensive cologne. "You were pissed about how she came at you the other day, and you wanted to make a point."

Guerrero held his ground and shrugged, making a clear effort to seem casual despite Clay's obvious anger. "I wasn't happy with her implications, but it's a free country. Ms. Thorn has a right to her opinion. In time, I hope to change her mind."

Clay pointed his finger in Guerrero's face. "No, you won't. You won't talk to her again even if she tries to talk to you, and you damned sure won't send any of your boys around to do your dirty work for you."

Guerrero backed off a step, then walked away from Clay, went to his desk, and sat looking at Clay. Clay had that sense again, that Guerrero was adding, subtracting, multiplying, doing whatever it took to total up everything he was seeing and hearing. "Is that a personal or a professional request?"

"Personal." Clay bared his teeth. "*Definitely* personal."

Guerrero leaned back in his cheap office chair. "I see." He let a beat pass. "I didn't know she was your woman."

Clay was too pissed to enjoy the *your woman* comment, but Guerrero was right on the money. Rylie was his, by God, and nobody like Guerrero would be going near her again. Ever. "The men who went to the ranch—"

"Won't be an issue again." Guerrero's voice rang with certainty, but Clay didn't sense any fear. Mild surprise, maybe, and an atypical stiffness to his posture, but no fear. "This visit is unnecessary, Sheriff. Levi Thorn, Rylie's brother, chased my men away before they could explain why I sent them, so that was the source of the misunderstanding. He came to town and spoke to me at the South showroom, and I thought we had struck a deal to call things even and let the situation rest between us."

Clay put both hands on Guerrero's desk and leaned toward the man. "Levi might have struck a deal. I didn't. You stay away from Rylie Thorn. You keep everyone you know, everyone who works for you, and everyone who even looks like you away from the Thorn Ranch. Anything else happens on that property—or off of it—if it involves Rylie, I *will* take it personally."

A few muscles in Guerrero's face twitched, and his words came out a little high and tight. "I heard you were such a clean man, a solid officer, unlike your predecessor. I never imagined you would threaten people."

Clay heard the growing understanding in the man's tone, and he eased off the desk. "There's a difference between threats and promises."

Guerrero stared straight at him, and Clay saw abject rage flash across his dark eyes, followed—weirdly enough—by something like understanding and grudging respect. Guerrero seemed to debate himself again for almost half a minute, then he spoke, this time in a level, low voice.

"Though I'm widowed, I'm still a family man. In all of my affairs, my children have no stake. I assume the families of your deputies— and your woman—also stay out of our business ventures. In my opinion, warriors are warriors, but families are off-limits."

Clay couldn't do anything but look at the guy. Was he serious? Did he honestly think Clay would buy that load of shit?

Guerrero seemed to sense Clay's dismissal, because he went the next step, leaning forward toward Clay to make his point. "My father didn't hold to that, and my brothers don't, but I'm an old-fashioned businessman, Sheriff Wayland. You might not agree with my activities, though they are perfectly legitimate, but I assure you, you will not have an issue with my methods. Douglas is my home, and home and family have meaning to me."

Clay didn't know what to say to that. The guy sure as hell seemed serious, but Clay couldn't let himself forget that he was speaking to a living, breathing chameleon. Guerrero was more than capable of saying exactly what he wanted to hear, and making it stick. Sociopaths were talented that way, charming on the surface, all the while waiting like a deranged cobra for the first chance to strike.

For now, all he could do was glare at the snake, study the snake, and try to learn its movements. He had a lot of intel to gather before he'd have a shot at lopping the head off this particular viper.

Clay clenched his fists, then made himself relax. "Fine. I'll trust that we have an understanding. Don't make me regret that."

Guerrero's nod was close to nonchalant, but he didn't quite pull it off. "Good day, Sheriff."

"Good day, Mr. Guerrero. I can see myself out."

It was late Monday afternoon by the time Clay drove his truck to the sheriff's office, still seething over his meeting with Guerrero. That silky little prick really got under his skin. Maybe he shouldn't have tipped his hand so hard about Rylie, but it wasn't like he was keeping her a secret. Soon enough, the criminal element in Douglas would know all about his interest in her—and he'd have to do what he did today a few more times.

Rylie would be off-limits. He'd keep making that clear through whatever means he had at his disposal.

Between that and the fact he hadn't been able to convince Rylie to go out with him during the week, Clay was in a pisser of a mood. How the hell was he supposed to wait until Friday to touch her again? His body throbbed just thinking about her. He guided his truck into his designated parking spot, and he clenched his jaw as he threw the vehicle into park, got out, and headed into the building that housed his office.

Even though he'd spent most of the day helping Levi Thorn put in the heater, Rylie had managed to avoid alone time with him at every turn. Finally, just before he took off to confront Guerrero, he'd told her he'd be there Friday night to take her with him to a dinner party at the mayor's home. He would pick her up at seven, end of story.

She hadn't spit at him, but damned close.

Apparently it was going to take some work to tame his little wildcat.

As for Levi Thorn, he'd turned the conversation so quickly Clay never got a chance to ask where he got the money for the water heater. Clay didn't figure him for a truck thief, though.

Rylie. She's clouding your judgment.

Possibility, definitely. But he didn't think so.

Clay only nodded to the receptionist as he passed her, then shut the door to his office a little too hard before settling in at his desk. Brogan's info was due—and sure enough, he found Rocky's e-mails the minute he signed on. He'd checked all these guys out before, when the cattle rustling started last year, but he'd checked through mainstream channels. Brogan was something other than mainstream, and he could find stuff normal reports and file searches withheld. Frowning, Clay went through the facts on each suspect, one by one.

First up was Zack Hunter, who wasn't really a suspect in Clay's mind, but Clay had spent too many years on the lines not to consider all his options—especially after Gary Woods, one of his own deputies, had gone bad right after he took the job. Who knew how many other rats were skulking around the Douglas woodpile? He hated that he had to consider law-enforcement officers as potential bad guys, but the situation on the border was what it was. Desperate times made people do desperate things.

But Hunter, he didn't seem to be one of the desperate people or one of the bad guys, either. Hunter had a virtually sterling record, first as a sheriff's deputy and then as an agent with ICE for the past decade. The only tarnish on the man's otherwise shiny profile was a drug deal that went bad while he was working undercover. Hunter had been seriously wounded and ended up in the hospital for a good month, and the perp got away with the dope. Internal Affairs had performed a thorough investigation, but Hunter had come up clean.

His frown deepening, Clay continued on down to the next name.

Guerrero. Brogan had written, "This bastard is six kinds of dirty," on the sheet above the printed facts. No record, just a long list of suspected activities, contacts, and off-the-books dealings. ICE and the DEA had files on him, and so did the FBI. Interestingly enough, though, there didn't seem to be any shift in the business patterns of the drug lord's car dealerships or cash movements in the last two months. Maybe the asshole actually wasn't involved in the thefts.

Wade Larson came next. Several tickets for speeding, and he'd been thrown in the Douglas City Jail once, after a drunken brawl where the local tavern had been trashed. Larson had come through for Clay when his own deputy had to be brought down, but he was well known to be a bit of a hothead and vigilante, taking matters into his own hands when it came to keeping UDAs—undocumented aliens—off his property. But the man had never been noted to use extreme measures and had not been cited for anything other than the brawl and tickets. Sometimes, jerks were just jerks, Clay knew. Still, he felt a moment of disappointment. Wade had been a good pick for something like this, stirring up the locals against UDAs, maybe to lobby for even stricter laws and restrictions.

Clay stroked his fingers over his mustache as he brought up the next suspect . . . and then his blood boiled.

When Levi Thorn was nineteen, he had beat the crap out of a kid who'd apparently tried to force Rylie to have sex in the backseat of his car at the drive-in. According to the police report, Levi had heard that Reggie Parker had been bragging he was going to "do the bitch."

Levi tracked them down and found Rylie trying to fight off the boy. Levi jerked the boy off of his sister, then punched the living daylights out of Parker, who'd ended up with stitches, a lost tooth, and a busted jaw. Because Levi had been nineteen, and Parker seventeen, Levi had been charged as an adult for assaulting a minor. The charges were cleared when the situation came to light.

Clay gritted his teeth. He hoped to hell that Levi had done some damage to that SOB who'd tried to rape Rylie. As far as Clay was concerned, he owed Levi for that one. Too damned bad it happened so long ago. This day and age, Reggie Parker would have been charged with attempted rape instead of being let go with an admonition to keep his urges under better control.

He read on, finding almost nothing of note that he didn't already know. Levi Thorn co-owned the Thorn Ranch with Rylie, and had been operating in the red for the past few years. He'd spent some time in the hospital a few years back for a spinal cord injury that took him out of the U.S. Marshals, but with therapy he was back on his feet. Bank records showed normal fluctuations in the ranch and personal accounts until a sudden influx of cash: ten grand deposited last week, then another ten grand a day ago.

Clay gave a low whistle. That was two good chunks of change

for a rancher whose only known source of income was a spread running in the red.

Clay narrowed his eyes.

What had Levi gotten himself into? Even if Clay continued to let himself believe he wasn't involved in stealing trucks, he sure as hell was involved in *something*.

Clay looked up from his documents and glanced out his door at the deputies in the main area. Blalock, Garrison, Quinn. He should have them all checked out after what happened with his former employee, Gary Woods, a gambler who got behind a cattle-rustling scheme. Lightning really could strike the same spot twice.

He swapped his screen view to a window and brought up some normal venues for checking records. Half an hour later, he knew that Blalock and Garrison had nothing but a few juvie beefs for intoxication and being out after curfew. Quinn—now that was interesting. Hazard Quinn had a few reprimands for not being in his assigned location a couple of times and, like Gary Woods, the former deputy now serving hard time, Quinn had filed for Chapter 13 bankruptcy protection the previous fall. Bad investments and an upside-down mortgage.

But hell, that was half the country.

And the poor man drove an ancient Gremlin for his personal car. Damned thing looked like it was held together with spit and rubber bands. If he was stealing trucks, he'd likely allow himself the luxury of a decent ride from the profits.

Clay's eyes drifted back to Levi Thorn's name, and he muttered, "Nothing for it, I guess. You and I need to talk."

* * *

"Oh, yes." Rylie sighed with pleasure as she eased into the old-fashioned footed tub and luxuriated in the warm bathwater. "That's more like it."

After a long, tiring Monday from hell, it was heaven to take a bubble bath. First she'd gotten into an argument with Levi because the big jerk refused to tell her where he'd gotten the money for the water heater; then one of the heifers had apparently eaten some locoweed and had to be put down; she'd ripped another good pair of jeans when she repaired the barbed-wire fence that had been cut again; and on top of that, the Bar One about fifteen miles down the road had lost a truck. The man watching it had been sent to the hospital for a concussion, and the hands had heard shots fired.

These assholes really weren't messing around.

Insurance had already agreed to send replacement funds for Thorn Ranch trucks, but she hated the idea of putting her ranch hands at risk guarding them. She needed a security system. Cameras, maybe alarms—but that was all too expensive to even contemplate. This crap needed to stop, and it needed to stop now.

"Not going to think about any of that right now." Rylie grabbed a loofah sponge from the soap tray and squirted her favorite vanilla musk gel on it. With energetic strokes, she scrubbed her skin until her body tingled.

It had been so long since they'd had hot water that she'd forgotten how wonderful it felt to relax in the tub after a hard day of ranch work. Even though Levi was keeping his trap shut on where he'd gotten the funds, she could almost forgive him for springing for the luxury of a new water heater. *Almost.*

Taking a deep breath of the vanilla-scented bubbles, she closed her eyes and leaned against the back of the old-fashioned footed tub, enjoying the silky feel of warm water against her skin. The sensual sensation made her think about Clay.

Everything made her think about Clay.

She wished she had his muscular body pressed into hers right this second, his breath hot against her neck, his hands busy with pleasing.

But for once, her own touch and mental fantasies failed to satisfy her. It was Clay that she wanted. . . . She *needed* to have the man's hands on her body. She'd had the real thing, and now her imagination just wouldn't do. At least till she got the man out of her system.

"Enough." With a frown she opened her eyes and scooted up in the tub. It really was starting to tick her off that she couldn't get him out of her mind. What the hell was the matter with her? He was just a man, nothing special.

Yeah, right.

Instead of enjoying a nice, leisurely bath, Rylie ended up rushing through the rest of it. She kept trying to shove Clay out of her thoughts, but the bastard kept returning, not leaving her alone.

When she'd toweled off, she threw on her old cotton robe, yanked a comb through her wet hair, and marched into her bedroom. She was pissed and obsessed, *not* a good combination. She'd put Clay off until Friday night and it was only Monday. How the hell was she going to make it until Friday without seeing him?

But at the same time, she wondered how he'd managed to convince her to attend a dinner with the mayor. The *mayor,* for crying out loud.

The piercing ring of her cell phone was like a screech through Rylie's mind. She checked the caller ID, but didn't recognize the number, and no name was shown. Rylie snatched up the phone, ready to take out her pent-up sexual frustration on the telemarketer who dared to interrupt her mental tirade. "Thorn."

"Yes. You are," Clay's deep voice rumbled over the phone. "Right in my side."

"Clay." Warmth flushed over Rylie, heating every cell, every pore on her body. "I'm what?" Why did her brain always take a hike around him?

"I can't quit thinking about you. I can't quit imagining you . . . in bed and out." His tone was throbbing with sensuality, stirring her in ways she hadn't thought possible over the phone. God, did he ever make her hot. "Sure you won't change your mind about dinner before Friday?"

It took all her resolve not to beg him to come over. Instead, she somehow managed to keep her voice light and teasing. "It's a busy week, cowboy."

"What are you doing right now?"

A spark of mischief skittered through her belly. She grinned and perched on the edge of her bed. "I'm lying in my bed . . . absolutely naked."

Clay sucked in his breath, and it was a good heartbeat before he responded. "You'd better be careful, little wildcat. I'll be there faster than you can make yourself happy."

Rylie pulled at the tie of her robe, his words giving her an idea. "Have you ever had phone sex?"

"Uh, no."

"Ah." She slid off the robe and settled against the pillows on her bed. "So you're a phone-sex virgin."

Clay gave a soft chuckle. "Been a long time since I was called that."

"Well, it's time you lose that cherry." Rylie cupped one of her breasts with her free hand. "I'll tell you what I'm doing. I'm playing with my nipples, imagining that you're sucking them."

"Damn, woman." Clay groaned, and she could visualize the raging desire in his expression. "I can picture your body, sleek and ready, just for me."

"Oh, yeah." Moisture flooded her core and cool air brushed her as she spread her legs. "Where are you right now?"

"In my study," he said, like he was gritting his teeth. "With a hard-on the size of Texas."

Rylie laughed. "Well, then. We need to do something about that."

"You coming over here, or am I going there?"

"Neither." She rubbed her hand up and down her flat belly. "Take off your clothes, cowboy."

A pause, and then he said, "Honey, I don't know what you do to me, but I can't believe I'm actually considering it."

"Just take off your clothes, big guy."

"Hold on." Clay grunted and she heard the rustle of fabric, the faint thump of boots on tile.

While she waited, Rylie closed her eyes and tweaked first one nipple, then the next as she pictured his hard-muscled body, naked and waiting for her. A part of her wanted to give in and meet with him before Friday. But she couldn't take the chance of starting to like the man *too* much, or give him the wrong idea—that they were anything more than friends and occasional lovers.

"Ready." Clay's voice interrupted her train of thought. "I need you here."

"Mmmmm." She squirmed on the bed, dying for the feel of him inside her. "Grab yourself and imagine that my tongue is licking over you, just like you're a supersized ice cream cone."

"And woman, do you ever have a talented tongue," he murmured. "My turn. I'm putting my fingers where they'll do the most good." Clay paused; she dipped her fingers into her slick folds. He lowered his voice and added, "Now taste yourself for me."

A small gasp escaped Rylie's throat at what he suggested and she hesitated. She'd smelled her own musk on her hand, and tasted herself on Clay's tongue, but lick her own fingers?

"Come on, honey." His groan was low and primal.

"All right, just for you." She smiled and brought her forefinger to her mouth and sucked on it with a smack loud enough for him to hear over the phone. "Mmmm. It's like tasting myself on you."

"Damn, but you make me hot." Clay's breathing was growing harsh. "I want you. I want you more than anything."

A thrill coursed through her, a heady feeling of power. The knowledge that she could turn this man on as much as he turned her on was addicting, like the most potent of drugs.

"Are you touching yourself?" Her fingers found her hot center and resumed the familiar motion that made her feel so good. "I'm touching myself, Clay."

"Yeah. I'd rather be the one doing that."

"That's good. So good." She clenched the phone tighter as her arousal grew. Her own breathing became more labored as her fingers worked harder, faster. "I'm picturing you. You're sliding into me, hard and fast."

"What if I took you from behind?" Clay murmured. "Would you like that?"

A wild moaned slipped through her lips at the thought of having him in total control, deciding her pleasure, making her ache. Her fingers stroked and stroked, bringing her closer to the peak.

"I can think of a lot of things you might like, Rylie." His tone was gruff. "Can you?"

"Yes, dammit." She had to force the words out as she began to climax. "With you, yes." The orgasm took hold of her body, her muscles clenching from head to toe. "Clay!" she shouted as she came. Her fingers continued, drawing out her orgasm, while her body shuddered and trembled.

Through the rush of blood in her ears she heard Clay's groan of release, his heavy breathing, and then his husky laugh.

"You're amazing." He sounded sated, but as if he could go another round or two. "No other woman on the face of God's green earth could make me do that on the telephone."

Laughter and pleasure filled Rylie. "Thanks for the great phone sex, cowboy," she murmured. And then she hung up on him.

Chapter 10

Rylie put on a pair of small gold hoop earrings, spritzed on her vanilla musk perfume, and then checked her appearance in the mirror. She rarely wore makeup, but wondered if today she should make an exception considering how she looked—like she was nervous or something. Her cheeks were so pale it made her freckles stand out across her nose.

What the hell, she might as well go for it. She settled for dusting a bronze blush on her cheekbones, a light coat of brown mascara, and lipstick in a burnt-cinnamon shade. And, why not?—a little sable liner along her lashes, just like the Avon lady had shown her.

Frowning at her reflection, Rylie smoothed the skirt of the strapless black dress that came to mid-thigh. It wasn't an expensive dress, but it had a classic look that supposedly made it appropriate for any occasion. Truth be told, she didn't give a damn about that—she just hoped that it would make Clay so out of his mind with lust that he'd want her as soon as he saw her.

It had been almost a week since she'd seen Clay, and she was regretting agreeing to go with him to the mayor's dinner. She wanted him so badly she didn't think she could wait until the dinner was over.

Her frown turned into a grin as she thought about how much fun it would be to find a secluded corner in the mayor's house, and tease Clay right there. With all their dirty talk on the phone every night this week, she was so hot for him she'd probably jump him the moment he arrived. She almost wished that tomorrow she didn't have to go to Skylar and Zack's reception. Clay had agreed to go with her, but right now she wanted him all to herself so that she could enjoy his body.

Rylie grabbed her black beaded handbag, tossed in the lipstick, and walked through the quiet house, wondering where it was that Levi had been going off to every night. He must have started working some kind of side job that he wasn't telling her about. How else could he have afforded the water heater? And why would he be so secretive about what he was doing?

When she reached the window that looked out onto the front yard, she pushed the curtain aside and peered through the clouded pane and into the night. A pair of headlights cut through the darkness, and headed up the dirt road to her ranch house. Her hand automatically went to her ear and she pulled at the gold earring.

Clay. Rylie held her purse tight to her belly with one hand, as if it could calm the sudden flutter there, and stepped back from the window. She took a deep breath and closed her eyes.

He's just a man. Nothing special.

The roar of a truck's engine came closer. She remained still, almost unable to move while she listened to the sound of gravel crunching under big tires . . . the engine cutting off . . . the slam of a door . . . and then the sound of heavy boots on her porch steps.

What's the matter with me?

The screen door creaked and then a loud knock sounded. Rylie's eyes flew open and she stared at the door. Why did it feel like everything would change if she walked through that door and into Clay's arms tonight?

Stop being so damn stupid!

Another knock jolted Rylie into action, and she moved forward and reached for the worn brass knob. When she opened the door, she almost forgot to breathe.

Clay was dressed in a black suit, his mouth curved into a sensual smile and his green eyes positively smoldering. He looked like he could have stepped out of the pages of some high-fashioned men's magazine.

"You're so gorgeous, honey." He reached for her, slid his fingers into her hair, and cupped the back of her head. "Damn, but I've missed you."

"Hey, sexy," was all she had a chance to say before he brought his mouth to hers. He moved his lips over hers in a soft and sensuous kiss that stole every bit of her remaining breath. A moan rose up within Rylie, and she barely realized she had wrapped her arms around his neck and pulled him tighter to her.

His kiss deepened, her thoughts spinning as she parted her lips and he slipped his tongue into her mouth. She welcomed him, drawing him deeper into her. Today he tasted of cinnamon and his own elemental flavor. Clay's arousal was clear, hard against her belly. Her core flooded at the thought of having that awesome length deep inside her again. It'd been too long since she'd had him.

Faintly she heard something clatter to the floor, but the whole world could come crashing down for all she cared. The only thing that mattered was the feel of this man in her arms, how good he tasted, his masculine scent, and the way he held her against him.

When he broke the kiss, he pressed his forehead to hers. Rylie opened her eyes to see his sexy smile so close to her lips. Feeling dazed and breathless, she swallowed, trying to calm the emotions rushing through her.

Not emotions—*lust*. That was all she felt for him . . . Lust.

He trailed his knuckles along her jaw line. "You ready to head on out, little wildcat?"

"Yeah." Her voice was barely a husky whisper.

Snap out of it! she shouted in her head.

Fixing a flirty smile on her face, Rylie pushed herself away from Clay. "I'm ready if you are."

"You don't know how ready I am." He winked, but then knelt and started picking up items from the floor—and Rylie realized what the clatter had been. She'd dropped her purse, scattering her ID, lipstick, and change all over the floor. Before she had a chance to help him, he had everything gathered up. "You carry a pocket-knife?" he asked as he dropped it into her purse and stood.

"I'm pretty handy with it." She shrugged and took her purse from him. "And it was a gift from someone who was like a mom to me. She lived down at the old Karchner Ranch, but she died a while back. Gina Garcia lived there for a while—you remember her."

Clay nodded.

Gina had taken off abruptly last year, and everybody had worried about her safety. She was the woman Clay sent Levi to track down to check on her, but that hadn't worked out well. Levi lost her in Utah, and never picked up her trail again.

"I think Levi was a little sweet on Gina. The for-sale sign at the Karchner place got taken down, but I haven't been by to see who's living there now. Too hard to go down there, you know? I always think of Mrs. Karchner."

"Ah." Clay glanced around the small living room. "Speaking of Levi, where is your brother?"

"Hell if I know." Rylie brushed a strand of hair behind her ear. "He's been gone every night and won't tell me where. I think he's got a side job and just doesn't want to tell me about it for some macho reason."

Something flickered in Clay's eyes, but then it was gone. "Let's go before I decide to forget all about the damn dinner." He brushed his lips over hers. " 'Cause the way you look tonight, honey, we'll be lucky if we even make it to the mayor's house."

"Who needs him anyway?" She flicked her tongue against the corner of his mouth, her naked skin aching beneath her dress.

He groaned and caught her face in his palms. "I brought a little something for you."

With a naughty grin, Rylie placed her hand against his package and felt its rigid length beneath his slacks. "You sure did, but I'd say that's more than a *little* something."

Clay captured her hand in one of his and held it to his chest, while his other hand dug into his suit jacket and pulled out a long jeweler's box.

Rylie's eyes widened and she tried to step back, but he held her hand too tightly against him. "I can't accept a gift from you, Clay." She swallowed as she looked up at him.

"Just open it." He placed the box in her free hand until she took it, and then released her other hand.

Curiosity won out, and she opened the box. Lying upon a bed of black velvet was a necklace, each link a tiny heart, and each heart with a diamond chip at its center. "It's gorgeous." She snapped the box shut and handed it back to him. "It's too expensive. You can't give me this and I can't accept it."

"Let's just see how it looks." He reopened the box and unhooked each end of the necklace from within its velvet nest.

"No." Rylie shook her head. "I've known you for less than two weeks. And I already told you, no commitment. Of any kind."

"I'm not asking for commitment." His smile was so erotic her nipples became diamond points against the thin fabric of her dress. "Just wear the necklace. Humor me, all right?"

Raising her chin, she gave him a mischievous smile. "Under one condition."

Clay quirked his brow. "What's that?"

"You have to promise to let me do what I want with that *other* thing you brought me."

His mouth curved up into a grin. "No problem."

"While we're at the mayor's house."

"Uh, no."

"Either that, or we have to do it." A devious feeling rose up within her. "Anywhere I say. Anytime. Somewhere very public."

Clay and Rylie arrived at the mayor's house promptly at seven. He glanced over at her in the passenger seat just as she bit her lower lip, and he realized that his feisty wildcat was nervous.

Well, good. Maybe she'd get that crazy public sex idea out of her beautiful little head. He couldn't believe he'd agreed to Rylie's condition—the woman was making him certifiably nuts. If he didn't watch it, his libido was going to get him into serious trouble.

Hell, he was already courting disaster by dating a suspect's sister. And after the new evidence that Deputy Quinn had reported, about seeing Levi riding after suspects in an interrupted burglary, it was looking more and more like Rylie's brother was in some deep shit. They'd know more after Quinn served the warrant at the bank and checked out that safety deposit box. Until then, he needed to let it all go and give Rylie his full attention.

He reached over and squeezed her hand. "Ready?"

A car passed, the headlights illuminating her delicate features as her eyes met his. She raised her chin, a proud tilt to her head. "What if I don't fit in here? I'm just a rancher—"

Clay caught her face in his hands and silenced her with a long, hard kiss. When he pulled away, he looked into her eyes that glittered in the near darkness. "Honey, you're smart and sexy . . . you fit me perfectly."

"But—"

He pressed his thumb against her lips, silencing her protest.

"Just be the beautiful and confident Rylie Thorn that I can't get enough of."

Clay helped her out of his truck, and she held his hand tight as they walked up to the home of Douglas mayor Eduardo Montaño, one of the biggest houses in the area. A well-known businessman even before becoming mayor, Montaño owned a popular Mexican restaurant in town. At one time Montaño had run for U.S. Congress but had lost to the incumbent.

Rylie's chin rose higher as a young man greeted them at the door, then escorted them into a formal living room already filled with guests. Clay squeezed her hand and felt her relax, as though his confidence was transferred to her. The mayor's home was decorated much as his restaurant was, in bold colors, with portraits of bullfighters and other décor that spoke of his Hispanic heritage. A quick check of the place told Clay one important thing: Guerrero wasn't present in the crowd. That would definitely make it a better night.

"Sheriff Wayland." Montaño approached them, holding out one hand. "It is good to see you again."

"Mayor Montaño." Clay grasped the mayor's hand in a firm grip, then released it to introduce Rylie. "Have you met Rylie Thorn? She and her brother own a ranch outside town."

Montaño clasped Rylie's hand and smiled. "A pleasure, señorita."

Her smile was radiant as she responded in kind to the mayor. Before Clay had the chance to say another word, Montaño took it upon himself to introduce Rylie to each of the other guests, which included council members and a couple of local business owners and their spouses. All Clay could do was follow like some third wheel, but every now and then Rylie would toss him a look that said *Don't forget your promise to take me in public,* and it was all he could do to keep from sporting a hard-on the entire evening.

Throughout the night, the way that the other men looked at Rylie, Clay couldn't decide whether he should want to kick their asses or stick out his chest with pride. She was a knockout in her tiny black dress and high heels, clearly the most beautiful woman there. Her hair shimmered like gold floss in the light of the chandeliers, and her brown eyes seemed bigger and more luminous than ever. The delicate chain of golden hearts and diamonds glittered with every move she made.

Truth be told, he had wondered what Rylie might come up with tonight as frank as she was in conversation. That was one of the things he loved about her, the way she spoke her mind without worrying about what others might think.

When they were seated for dinner, Clay and Rylie found themselves in the middle of one side of the table set for twelve.

"I've never been to such a fancy dinner," Rylie whispered to Clay as they were served cold gazpacho in footed silver bowls. "I'm afraid I'm going to do something stupid."

"You'll do fine, honey." He settled his hand on her knee beneath the tablecloth, enjoying her slight gasp as he moved his fingers to the warm flesh inside her thigh. "Just do what I do."

"All right." She smiled and moved her hand to his lap, right where it counted. "Like that?"

Clay's cock jerked and hardened at her touch, and he fought the urge to see if the people seated to either side of them could see what she was doing to him. He lowered his lids, his gaze burning into hers. "Eat your dinner."

She spoke so softly that he almost had to read her lips, as she said, "I'd rather have you for a main course."

He damn near groaned out loud at the thought of those lips and that soft mouth going down on him. The councilman on Rylie's other side took that moment to ask her a question, and her teasing brown eyes were drawn from Clay.

As they ate dinner, conversation ranged from politics to various other problems that plagued the border community. Rylie made it a point to torture Clay with a hand on his lap, or sliding off her shoe and running her silken foot along his ankle. At one point she even leaned in, her vanilla musk scent sweeping over him as she whispered, "I want to fuck you now."

Clay just about choked on his mouthful of grilled salmon. He retaliated by sliding his fingers along the inside of her thigh, planning to rub his fingers along the crotch of her panties—only to have his fingers come in contact with warm, bare skin. His erection hardened to the point he'd thought for sure it would thrust right through the material of his dress slacks.

When the topic of truck thefts came up, Clay tried to head it off with, "We're working on it," but each person at the table seemed to have some comment.

"Well, something needs to be done, and soon," Rylie added to the conversation. Clay tensed beside her.

Eduardo Montaño's eyes rested on her. "What would you suggest?"

She set her fork on the edge of her plate, her gaze steady as it met the mayor's. "It's obvious that it can't be completely an out-side job." Conversation around the table quieted as Rylie contin-ued, "The thieves know who's home and who isn't, good times to strike, times to stay away . . . I believe it's someone familiar with folks in the area."

Montaño nodded. "Do you think it could be anyone you know?"

Clay was practically holding his breath as he watched Rylie brush a strand of hair behind her ear, a troubled look crossing her face. "I can't imagine it would be any of the ranchers in our area. They're all good people, and most of them have been hit. But whoever it is, the law should lock them up for good once the bastard's caught."

Murmurs of agreement came from around the table, and Clay took the opportunity to ask what everyone thought about the Cardinals' chances of making the play-offs that year.

"Cardinals?" Rylie scoffed, her brown eyes meeting his. "Have you had a look at the way their defense has been playing lately?"

"The 49ers are going to put the Cardinals away in the next game," Montaño agreed.

While the banter continued, Clay studied Rylie, who passion-ately participated in the debate. He hadn't even realized that she was a football fan. How much more of a perfect woman could he have asked for?

He just hoped to God that Rylie wasn't going to hate him if he ended up having to arrest her brother.

When a decadent chocolate mousse was served for dessert, Rylie found her opportunity. Or rather, she made it.

"Ow," she said, just loud enough to be heard over the appreciative murmurs around the table. "Something's in my eye."

"Can I do something for you?" Montaño asked as Rylie held her hand over her eye.

"Just point me to the bathroom, and I'll take care of it." She started to push back her chair, but Clay was already standing and pulling it out for her.

"Do you mind helping me?" she asked him, keeping the one eye squeezed shut.

"Of course." His expression was concerned, yet the flare in his green eyes told her he knew she was up to something. Clay pressed his hand to the small of her back as he guided her across the massive house and into the opulent rose-scented bathroom.

The moment they were inside, she locked the door and wrapped her arms around his neck and grinned. "We had a bargain, lawman."

He groaned, but his big hands gripped her hips, the heat burning through her thin dress like a pair of branding irons. "You're such a little minx."

"Enough talk." Her hands moved to his belt, and a small thrill charged through her at the feel of his already huge length beneath his dress slacks. She was so turned-on she couldn't wait to get him inside her. "Just get on with it, big guy."

Clay yanked up her dress and rubbed her bare ass with his palms as she freed his length and pushed his slacks down around his hips. A sigh of sheer lust escaped her as she slid her fingers up and down his erection.

He grasped her ass and raised her up onto the marble countertop, and she jerked her attention to his face. His eyes burned a deep, passionate brown as he pushed her thighs apart and pressed himself against her.

"Damn, you drive me crazy, woman." He brushed himself against her swollen folds, then stroked her, easing toward her wet depths. "What I'd do for you."

"Then do it now." Rylie moaned and braced her hands on the countertop, the marble cold and erotic beneath her bare ass.

In one smooth motion, Clay drilled her. She gasped at the incredible sensation of having him fill her again. Damn, but she'd missed him inside her this week.

"Oh, God, that feels good. So, so good." She watched him moving in and out, loving every second. "More. I need *more*."

He grasped his hands beneath her knees, drawing her up and widening her to take more of him. Harder and harder he thrust inside her, their breathing coming in harsh gasps.

"Yes, that's it." She wished she could get her hands on his hard muscled body. Wished she could rake her nails down his back.

"I'm going to come, honey." His voice was low and hoarse. "Come with me."

"I'm ready." Rylie's breathing was labored as she felt her muscles begin to clench. "Now, Clay."

Just as she felt a scream rise in her throat, Clay placed his mouth over hers. His kiss was strong and fierce, swallowing her cries and feeding her his own as their bodies jerked and throbbed against one another. For a moment, they remained in that intimate embrace, the smell of passion rising like heady fog around them.

Clay's eyes locked with hers, their chests rising and falling with equally labored breaths. And then he smiled, the look in his eyes purely male sexual satisfaction. Rylie couldn't help but return his smile.

"Damn, that was fun," she said, with an intense desire to giggle.

He grinned and pressed a kiss to her forehead. "Talk about an understatement."

When they both had caught their breath, they cleaned up. Rylie rubbed her eye to make it look red, like she'd really had something in her eye.

Clay shook his head as he checked his own appearance in the mirror and then looked down like he was making sure there was no wet spot on his fly. "I can't believe we just did that in the mayor's house."

"A deal's a deal," she murmured as she reached up and kissed him.

Chapter 11

Rylie woke the following morning with Clay's arms wrapped tight around her, one hand cupping her breast. He had a leg hooked over hers, and his face was buried in the crook of her neck, his warm breath brushing over her skin. It felt so good waking up with him . . .

Wait. What the hell was she doing? Twice now she'd broken her no-spending-the-night rule. Twice with the same man, no less.

When he'd asked her to spend the night after they'd left the mayor's house, she caved, plain as could be. Maybe she should have seen him during the week, 'cause she would have gotten him a little more out of her system. As it was, she couldn't seem to satisfy her craving for his taste, his smell, or the feel of him deep inside her.

Yeah, that was it. The sex. When she'd had enough of him she'd break it off like she always did.

A contented sigh eased through her as she allowed herself to relax in his arms. Her muscles felt the good ache of a long, passionate night, and the smell of their sex surrounded her, filling her senses.

Clay stirred, rubbing himself all along her backside, and desire flared all over again. More than desire. More than want. Need curled through her belly. Damn, but she had to get through this quick before she fell in lo—

No. Not going there. Ever. I'm not an idiot like either of my parents were.

His lips and tongue began a moist trail down the curve of her neck. "Good morning, beautiful."

"Hi, Sheriff." Rylie shivered and closed her eyes, trying to fight off the deeper feelings of intimacy surging through her. Feelings that she didn't believe in, that she couldn't allow herself to acknowledge.

"I think I like waking up with you in my arms," Clay's husky voice murmured, and she had to bite her tongue not to agree. He squeezed and flexed the sweetly tender flesh of her breast, and her nipple sprang to life beneath his touch.

"Well, don't get used to it," Rylie replied instead, but her voice wavered as her arousal grew.

"Don't count on that, honey." He rubbed the inside of his thigh along her hip while rubbing his erection along her backside. A moan escaped and she arched into his hand.

Before she had a chance to catch her breath, Clay rolled her over and slid between her thighs. He propped his arms to either side of her, his brown hair tousled and his morning beard making him appear dark and dangerous. He just looked down at her with sleepy morning arousal in his green eyes, and that sexy smile that took her breath away.

And something more that she definitely did not want to see.

Rylie squirmed, wrapping her legs around his hips, and tried to reach for him. "Just get busy already."

"Uh-uh." In a quick movement he grabbed both her wrists and pinned them over her head. "Let's take this slow and easy."

His mouth captured her protest and turned it into a moan that burned through her soul. His kiss was gentle but demanding, encouraging and insistent all at once.

Rylie couldn't think any longer, she could only feel . . . his lips, soft yet firm against hers, the rough scrape of his stubble against her cheeks and her mouth, the taste and smell of him that flooded her senses.

She whimpered, clamping her legs tighter around his hips, pressing his erection to her belly. But he ignored her body's pleas, torturing her with the kiss, filling her mouth with his tongue and his taste.

When he finally raised his head, she couldn't seem to catch her breath. He studied her with heavy-lidded eyes, one hand still pinning both her wrists above her head, the other stroking her hair from her face.

"You are so beautiful, honey." His voice was a sensual purr that shimmered through her body in waves, a sensation she'd never felt before.

"Please." She swallowed, not knowing what she was begging him for. To touch her and chase all her thoughts away? To stop making her feel like she could fall in . . .

No. She just wanted him to take her good and hard.

Clay smiled as though he'd heard the thoughts she wouldn't allow herself to finish. "You're mine, Rylie Thorn." His expression turned positively possessive, even predatory. "Don't think for one moment you aren't."

She shook her head, but he only smiled again and stilled her with another soul-searing, spine-tingling, world-ending kiss. Everything melted around her and she was only aware of his lips and tongue against her skin as he moved his mouth to her ear, dipping inside and then nipping her lope with his teeth.

"Clay." Rylie could hardly catch her breath, and forget about being able to form a single thought. "Please."

"Tell me what you want." His mouth, tongue, and teeth continued down her neck to her shoulder. "What do you need?"

"You . . . I need you inside me." She arched her back and cried out as he captured her nipple between his teeth and gently bit. "Stop making me wait."

"That's not what you need." His tongue laved her nipple, first hard, then gentle. "Tell me what you really need."

"What . . . what the hell are you talking about?" Damn, but she couldn't even think, she had to have him so badly.

He moved to her other nipple, giving it the same attention he'd showered on the first. Laving it, sucking it, nipping at it. "This isn't just about sex anymore, honey."

She barely realized he had released her hands as he moved his mouth down her flat belly, over her shaved mound and to her leg. "Yes." Rylie gasped as Clay's tongue flicked along the inside of her thigh. "I mean, yes, it is just about sex."

"Uh-uh." He continued swirling his tongue close to her swollen lower lips, but not pressing inside like she wanted him to. "You can deny it all you want, but this is a hell of a lot more."

"Damn you, Clay Wayland." Emotion and sensation whirled through Rylie as he tortured her with his words and tongue. "I told you I've never believed in commitment, or anything that goes along with it."

He raised himself up on his elbows and his mouth quirked into a grin, his expression confident. "But that was before you met me." He trailed a finger down her shaved skin and touched her hot spot, and she nearly came off the bed with the intense sensations shooting through her.

Before she could tell him what an arrogant bastard he was, he lowered his head and lapped at her, and she cried out from the excruciating pleasure. Oh, God, did his tongue ever feel good as he licked and sucked, bringing her close to orgasm, and then backing off and starting the whole thing over again. She slid her hands in his thick hair, welcoming the distraction from their conversation, not wanting to examine the feelings growing inside her.

"Clay, please." Her hands clenched tighter in his hair, her thighs trembling from the orgasm that was almost about to overtake her. "Please let me finish."

A growl rumbled from his chest as he slid both palms under her ass and buried his face hard against her.

Rylie screamed, her body jerking hard with every aftershock of her release. It seemed as if her climax would never end. Her eyesight blurred, and she couldn't see or hear, only feel. He continued on, sucking and licking until a second orgasm sent her reeling beyond the first.

For a moment, she could only stay there, perched on a precipice of sensations, unable to move. Gradually, she came back down, her breathing harsh, heart pounding and blood rushing in her ears. Her vision cleared and her awareness of the world around her returned just as Clay eased up her body and propped himself above her. He watched her, an almost serious expression on his handsome face.

Lowering his weight so that he was pressed against her, he reached up and stroked her hair out of her face. "My little wildcat."

"No." She shook her head, not wanting him to voice the emotion she saw in his eyes. "Don't go there."

Clay smiled. "Whether you want to hear it or not, I'm going to tell you exactly where we're headed." He trailed his thumb along her lips, a slow and sensuous movement that caused her to catch her breath. "I'm in love with you, Rylie Thorn."

"You haven't known me long enough to say that." Her lower lip trembled. "It's just the sex. We're good in bed."

"Listen to me." Clay put his hand over her mouth, his calloused fingers warm against her lips. "I knew from the moment you walked into my office. You're my woman."

Rylie widened her eyes and tried to speak, but he only pressed his thumb tighter to her mouth.

"I know you need time, and I'll give it to you." His smile was gentle, yet determined. "But you're not going to keep pushing me away, and you're not going to keep pretending this is all about sex." She tried to shake her head, but he moved his hands and caught her face between his palms. "You'd better get used to it, honey, 'cause you're my woman, and I'm your man."

His kiss was hard and possessive, melting away her automatic denial. She gave in to the sensations, and somewhere deep in her heart, she reveled in the knowledge that this man had declared his love to her. That out of any woman he could have chosen, he loved *her.*

God. She was losing her mind. And the next thing she knew, she'd be losing her heart, too.

"This isn't just sex, Rylie." He positioned himself at the entrance to her core, his eyes locked with hers. "I'm making love to you."

Clay plunged inside her and she automatically raised her hips to meet him. He was such a perfect fit. And somehow it felt more intense, more pleasurable than it ever had before. As if knowing he loved her made their sex even better.

Making love.

Unable to take her eyes from his as he thrust with slow and deep strokes, Rylie bit her lip to hold back any words that might decide to spill out on their own. He smiled and brought his mouth to hers, licking her lip where she was biting it. She wrapped her arms around his neck, holding on tight as she opened up to his tongue, and maybe even to the sweet emotions sweeping through her heart and soul.

This time her orgasm came out of nowhere. Fireworks exploded in her mind, brilliant colors and flashes of light that rocked her straight to her core. The walls of her channel contracted, gripping him with every pulse of her release.

"I love you, Rylie," Clay murmured, his words uneven with his harsh breathing. And then he groaned with his orgasm, throbbing inside her as he came.

He rolled over onto his side, pulling her with him and staying tight inside her. He held her to his chest, their sweaty flesh pressed close, enveloping her in his strong arms. "You're mine, little wild-cat. All mine."

While Rylie sat beside him on the drive to the Flying M Ranch right before noon on Saturday, Clay wondered what was going on in her gorgeous head. He had a good idea that she was sorting out her feelings for him, yet trying to keep from acknowledging them. But as far as he was concerned, it was only a matter of time.

Of course, if he ended up having to arrest her brother, that might put a bit of a damper on their relationship.

She'd been fairly subdued when he drove her to the Thorn Ranch to change and get ready for the MacKenna-Hunter shin-dig. Levi Thorn had been there, but the man hadn't had much to say, and he seemed to have a lot on his mind. Clay liked Levi, and his gut told him that Thorn was a good man. But from experi-ence, Clay knew too well how a good man could end up in a bad situation and not know how to dig himself out.

Outside, the spring day was partly cloudy, but it didn't look like it would rain, at least not until late evening. Acres of dry grass rolled by on the two-mile drive, populated by herds of cattle. Clay gritted his teeth at the thought of what he might have to do soon. A little more evidence and he wouldn't have a choice.

Rylie seemed to tense the closer they got to the Flying M Ranch, and one hand moved to her neck to play with the hearts-and-diamonds necklace he'd convinced her to wear. She clenched her other hand so tight on her lap that her knuckles whitened against her denim skirt. Her blond hair shone in the sunlight and her chocolate eyes looked so big she appeared younger than she was. She had flawless skin, a natural beauty that didn't need makeup, and the freckles across her nose were just damn irresistible.

Clay took one hand off the steering wheel and placed it over hers. "You all right, honey?"

"Why wouldn't I be?" She gave a forced smile. "It's just a party."

He turned his attention back to the dirt road as he made the turn into the Flying M Ranch. "It bothers you that your friend has gotten married."

"I'm happy for Skylar."

"But you're worried about her for the same reason you're worried about us." He glanced at Rylie as she raised her chin, a defiant look on her face.

"You know my history, Clay," she said as he looked back to the road.

"It's not *your* history. Can't you get that through your thick little head?" He gave her a crooked grin. "It's a beautiful head, but damn thick."

Rylie's lips twitched. "You'd better watch it, or I'll come up with something really good to do to you while we're at the barbeque."

"Uh-oh." Clay shook his head as he guided the truck up to the MacKenna house. "You've got that look in your eyes again. Don't tell me you're gonna try to corner me in the bathroom again."

She reached over and rubbed him through his jeans. "Oh, just you wait. I'll think of something even better."

Clay groaned as he pulled the truck alongside a row of vehicles parked in the massive front yard. Obviously it was going to be one hell of a party—there had to be fifty vehicles there. Off to the right, to the side of the barn and extensive corrals, huge awnings had been pitched, and folks milled around, chatting and carrying plates heaped with food.

"Looks like everyone and their mother is here," Rylie said as he opened the door and climbed out.

He took her hand as she followed him out the driver side door, enjoying the feel of her small fingers within his. Her skirt hiked up and his body warmed at the thought of what was under that skirt—nothing but bare skin, just waiting for him to touch.

"Later, Sheriff." With a naughty smile, Rylie pulled her skirt lower, hiding that delicious prize. "If you're a good boy, I might just let you sample some."

Clay groaned and swatted her on the ass while he slammed the door shut. "If you're not a good girl, I'm gonna have to turn you over my knee and spank you."

She grinned up at him as he draped his arm around her shoulders. "You keep promising and not delivering."

Even though he was determined that she take their relationship seriously, he was glad to see her feisty personality and sass had returned. He held her close as they walked toward the crowd, the sound of voices and laughter filling the warm early-spring air. Children played Frisbee and football out in the field, and to the side of the tents a few folks apparently had a hot game of horseshoes going on. A faint breeze carried with it smells of grilled beef and roasted chicken, along with the tangy scent of barbeque and spice.

Rylie was her animated self as she greeted people she knew and was introduced to those she didn't. Clay could hardly tear his gaze from her beautiful smile long enough to do his own share of socializing. It felt good to be with her anywhere they went.

But damn, he couldn't wait to get her alone again.

Chapter 12

Rylie made polite talk as she worked her way through the crowd with Clay at her side. They stopped to talk with Wade Larson for a moment. Rylie was almost surprised to see him, since he'd been after Skylar himself for so long, but the man was his usual half-surly, down-home-boy self.

Everyone seemed to want to make small talk with Rylie and Clay, but she was dying to find her best friend to see if she was really as happy about being married as she'd seemed all these months. It couldn't last—Rylie knew that—but the months were starting to stack up. Surely, Skylar wasn't as thrilled as she had been, right?

When Deputy Quinn greeted them, it was all Rylie could do to patiently wait by Clay's side while they bullshitted about one thing or another.

Finally, Rylie spotted Skylar MacKenna-Hunter in the crowd and her heart rate picked up. She asked Quinn to excuse them as she grabbed Clay's hand and then led him toward where her friend stood with her new husband. They were across the way, standing near where a dance would be later that evening. A makeshift dance floor had been laid out beneath a massive tent, with speakers and other soundstage equipment for a live band.

Clay's hand tightened around Rylie's as they walked toward the newlyweds. Skylar seemed more beautiful than ever, her hair tumbling down her back in a fall of auburn, a radiant smile on her face. Zack was watching Skylar with pride in his eyes, and a look that said, *This is my woman.*

Not for the first time, Rylie had to acknowledge that Skylar's husband was certainly a handsome man, *although not nearly as gorgeous as my man.*

The thought made Rylie falter and only Clay's grip on her hand kept her moving forward until they reached her friend.

When Skylar turned and saw Rylie, delight filled her expression. "Where the heck have you been keeping yourself these last few weeks, sweet pea?"

"I still can't believe you went and did it, girlfriend." Rylie hugged Skylar tight, inhaling her friend's familiar orange blossom scent. "Are you keeping that man in line?"

Skylar laughed as she pulled away. "It's an uphill battle," she replied with a grin at Zack.

Nope. No sign of waning joy. No sign of sneaking, creeping misery. All Rylie could see in her friend's face was happiness.

"Well, be sure and call me if you need any help." Rylie turned from Skylar to face Zack, and poked her finger at his chest. "Now listen good, cowboy. You treat my best friend right, or I'm gonna kick your ass."

Amusement sparked in his gray eyes as he gave her a solemn nod. "Of course, sweet pea."

"Only Skylar is allowed to call me that." Rylie planted her hands on her hips and gave him a pretend glare. "And if you don't behave, I'll tell everyone what her pet name is for you."

Zack cast Skylar a look over Rylie's head. "You didn't."

Skylar reached up and planted a kiss on his cheek. "Sorry, baby. I did." He rolled his eyes and Skylar laughed.

"Congratulations, Hunter." Clay stepped forward and offered his hand to Zack. "Snagged yourself one beautiful woman."

"That I did." Zack grinned and clasped Clay's hand and then released it. "I hear you caught one of your own," he added, with a wink at Rylie.

Clay hooked his arm around her shoulders and pulled her close. "Got that right."

"Well, he'd like to think so." Heat flushed Rylie's cheeks and she elbowed him in the side. "Trust living in a small community to spread crazy rumors."

"Now what was Denver telling me?" Clay said to Zack. "That the night you decided to get married, you tossed your woman over your shoulder and carted her off to Vegas?"

"Yup." Zack caught a handful of Skylar's auburn hair and tugged on it. "Wasn't about to let her get away."

Clay looked down at Rylie with a teasing grin on his face. "So that's how it's done."

She gave a loud sniff and folded her arms across her chest. "Try it and you won't be walking straight, Sheriff Wayland."

Zack chuckled and laughter glimmered in Skylar's light green eyes.

"When's Trinity coming home from her delayed honeymoon?" Rylie asked, anxious to change the subject. "She and Luke are in Australia, right?"

"Yeah, but the first week she's scheduled to be all over the place, working in public relations for her new software company." Skylar's grin seemed to light up the room. "The second week is the one she'll really get to enjoy—or should I say it's the week she'll really get to enjoy Luke. We'll probably have to do a reception like this for her, somewhere down the road."

Rylie reached out and squeezed her friend's arm. "I'll be here for that one, too."

God, it was weird. Both of the MacKenna sisters had gotten married. Her old world had changed in what felt like five seconds, and she hadn't seen it coming.

"Way to go, Hunter," a deep masculine voice interrupted, and Rylie's eyes cut to Noah Ralston, another sweet-talking hunk who lived in the local area. Noah gave Skylar that sexy grin that used to make Rylie's heart flutter. "'Bout time someone roped in that gal."

As Noah congratulated the newlyweds, Rylie's gaze went from Noah to Zack, and then rested on Clay. Good Lord, talk about a trio of handsome male specimens. All were around the six-foot range, all big and muscular, and all drop-dead gorgeous cowboys.

Yet the only man who gave her any kind of thrill now was Clay. It was as if he filled her senses, fit her life in ways she never dreamed a man could.

Somehow the thought both frightened and comforted her, a

strange and unsettling feeling that she couldn't decide what to do with. The weight of his arm around her shoulders felt *right,* and she found herself wanting to lean into him. Wanting to draw strength from him and let him lead. Wanting to not always have to be the willful woman she prided herself on being.

If she allowed herself to give in to these feelings, would she be giving up her own identity?

Rylie pushed the thoughts to the back of her mind. She couldn't deal with them now. The thoughts were too new, too fresh, too . . . alien.

Her gaze roamed the crowd and she spotted her brother talking to a curvy woman with black hair and a beautiful smile. The way the woman was looking at Levi, and the slightly goofy expression that was on her brother's face, made Rylie snap to attention.

"I'll be right back," she said to Clay. Before he could respond, she slipped out from under his arm and made a beeline for Levi.

He was making such goo-goo eyes at the gal that he didn't even notice Rylie's approach, so she butted right in. "Hi." She grinned as she stuck out her hand, offering it to the brunette. "I'm Rylie. Levi's sister."

The woman grasped Rylie's hand, her smile warm and friendly. "Chloe Somerville. I'm a friend of Skylar's from college—just came in for the reception, but I've been in Bisbee for about a month now." Chloe released Rylie's hand and turned her dark eyes on Levi, who had a sheepish look on his face. "Your brother's mentioned you quite often."

Before Rylie could respond, *Funny, but I've never heard of you,* Chloe hooked one finger on the back of a wheelchair beside her, drawing Rylie's eyes to a boy of about nine or ten years of age. She'd been so focused on Levi and Chloe that she hadn't even noticed him until that moment.

"This is my son David." Chloe's look was one of an adoring mother as she stroked his dark hair from his eyes. "He has a recent spinal-cord injury. Levi has been helping him with his therapy by teaching him how to ride, and he ramped our rental cottage to make things easier. I'm buying the old Karchner place, so he's been working on getting it modified for David, too. It's older . . . some of the doorways are too narrow, and of course, there are steps everywhere . . . Sorry, I'm babbling."

The Karchner place. Why does it seem like destiny keeps taking my family back to that old ranch?

Rylie blinked, her gaze darting from Chloe and David to that big lug of a brother who was just standing there, his face three shades brighter. Luckily for her, Rylie was rarely at a loss for words. Usually, the only one who could do that to her was Clay.

She knelt on the ground, at David's level, and extended her hand to him. "Is Levi being nice to you? 'Cause if he's not, I can take him on. Even though he's bigger and older than me, I can still whoop on him."

David grinned as he took Rylie's hand and gave her a surprisingly firm handshake. "He's pretty okay." The boy lowered his voice, and added, "Even though I think he's got the hots for my mom."

"David!" Chloe gave her son a playful swat on his shoulder, a mortified look on her pretty face.

Rylie laughed and caught her brother's embarrassed expression. "I've never seen you blush before, big guy."

He shook his head and winked at Chloe. "Obviously, I don't keep this kid busy enough when I'm there." Levi ruffled David's hair. "Partner, I think you need a few more turns around the corral on Dumpling."

The boy rolled his eyes. "Dumpling is a baby's horse. When can I ride Shadow Warrior?"

Rylie stood and dusted off her bare knees. "That's a lot of animal, even for me, and I've been riding since I could walk. I'd hold off a little longer on saddling him up and taking a ride." She placed her hands on her hips and tilted her head. "Now, Sassafras would be a good step up. That mare's well trained and gentle as can be. Sass is mine, but I wouldn't mind you riding her when Levi says you're ready."

"Cool!" David's eager gaze shot to Levi. "Can I?"

"Hmmm." Levi rocked back on his heels and stroked his chin with a look of serious consideration. "Not much longer, and I think you'll be ready. If your mom can bring you down to my barn for once, we'll give it a go."

David pumped his small fist in the air. "All right!"

Rylie laughed. "I'd better get on back to that bunch over there. If I don't, Skylar's likely to tell Clay stories about me that I'd rather she keep to herself." She gave David a grin. "Now, you make sure you come see me and Sass soon, ya hear?"

A broad smile creased David's face from ear to ear. "You bet!"

As she turned to leave, she lightly punched Levi's biceps. "You and me. We're gonna talk when I get you alone."

He just shook his head and smiled. "Go on and get out of here, Ry."

Cool air chilled her cheeks as she walked toward where Clay and the newlyweds were still standing. Boy, when she got home, she was going to have a talk with that brother of hers, and find out why the hell he'd been keeping secret his relationship with Chloe and David Somerville.

As Rylie headed back to find Clay, she passed by a gap between two of the tents. Masculine voices came from behind the tents, tense with a lot of wariness and searing. It piqued her curiosity. She paused, trying to identify them. In the days before Clay, she would have taken a peek, just to see if they were good-looking or not. Now she could care less.

She shook her head, sure she was losing her mind. All she could think about was one man. Hell, she wasn't even interested in watching anyone else have sex or any of the other kinky things involving multiple partners that she used to fantasize about and thought she'd wanted to try. Compared to sex with Clay, that other stuff seemed downright . . . boring.

Yup. She was losing it.

She started to walk away when she caught a familiar voice saying, ". . . Right below Larson's north range water tower."

Rylie stopped in midstep. Now *that* was intriguing. They were describing the area close to where Levi had found their fence cut.

"Twenty-one hundred hours. Get your ass there early."

She didn't recognize that voice, though it sounded a tad familiar, but the other voice . . .

"What about Wayland?"

That voice. She felt a creeping chill in her gut. It couldn't be.

"Ah, hell. He's too busy chasing Thorn."

Rylie waited. Then the second voice growled, "You better be right."

The chill in her depths became a deep freeze.

It couldn't be Reggie Parker.

Still in Vegas, last time Levi checked. And it had been years since she'd heard him talk. High pitched, almost whining, definitely entitled. There's no way he would have been invited to Skylar's reception.

No, Rylie thought, *it couldn't be Reggie.*

She walked away, fast, shoving her fears and worries to some other place inside her. It made no earthly sense for Reggie Parker to be in town, much less at this reception. Who would have brought a weasel like that to Skylar's? And why would he risk Levi catching sight of him and finishing the beating he started all those years ago?

It wasn't Reggie. That's it. Period.

It was just somebody that sounded like him. Rylie decided to believe that in the front of her mind . . . but in the back of her mind, she wondered—and she worried.

While they mingled with the other guests at the reception, it had been all Clay could do to not just grab Rylie and take her off to a hidden corner in the barn.

As it was, he was forced to perform the social niceties while Rylie teased him. Whenever she could get away with it without being noticed by other people, she'd brush her hand over his cock, rub her breasts along his arm, or perform any number of other taunts that were about to drive him out of his mind.

Come sunset, Clay and Rylie were sitting with Skylar and Zack at one of the tables surrounding the dance floor. The band started up and the newlyweds were dragged out onto the floor to dance a slow one alone before everyone else joined in. Folks with children had headed on home, leaving mostly couples sitting at the tables around the dance floor. Lamps had been arranged to provide romantic lighting, and Clay thought the ambience was just exactly right.

While they watched Skylar and Zack dance, Clay rubbed his fingers along Rylie's arm and felt her shiver beneath his touch. Candlelight flickered within the hurricane lamp at the center of the table, the soft glow illuminating her golden features.

"You ready to go, honey?" he said, hoping like hell she'd agree.

"Let's dance first." She moved her lips to his ear and murmured, "Then we can go home and play."

His groin tightened as he slid his hand beneath the tablecloth and eased his fingers up the inside of her thigh, knowing this time he'd reach bare skin if he kept on going. It was dark, and they were alone at the table, so he wasn't worried about anyone noticing what he was doing. "Sure you want to wait?"

Rylie's smile was wicked, and she spread her thighs a little to allow him access. "We haven't done anything naughty here. Yet."

Clay's body burned with the need to possess her. His fingers eased up beneath her short skirt, reaching the smooth lips that were already warm and wet. "Let's get out of here so I can have you for dessert."

Her eyelashes swept down as his hand cupped her shaved mound.

"Just one dance." She moaned as he slipped a finger into her folds. "Clay. Someone might see."

"Maybe you shouldn't have been teasing me all night." He increased his motions, his finger sliding back and forth. The way her thighs trembled around his hand, he knew she was close to the edge, even though he'd barely touched her. "Open your eyes."

She obeyed and glanced around at the empty tables as he continued to stroke her. A new song had started, and practically everyone else was on the dance floor. "Oh, God. I'm almost there."

"That's it." Damn, what he would give to take her behind the tent and have her now. "Come for me, honey."

The climax scalded Rylie in a hot rush and her body jerked against his hand. She bit down on her lip, holding back her cry, and leaned against Clay's shoulder, trembling with every stroke of his finger. "Stop." Her voice came out husky as she spotted her friends. "Skylar and Zack are coming back."

Clay stilled his finger, but kept it in place as the newlyweds returned. She reached down to try to pry his hand away, but he wasn't budging. Her entire body continued to throb and pulse, the feeling seeming to amplify as Skylar and Zack seated themselves at the table.

"Are you two going to dance?" Skylar leaned up against Zack as he brought his arm around her. "Or are you planning to sit here all night?"

"We're—" Rylie started just as Clay flicked his finger against her sensitized nub, and she damn near came unglued. Furious heat engulfed her and she sat bolt upright while trying to yank Clay's finger away from her at the same time. "We were just about to."

She cut Clay a glare that said, *Just you wait till I get you alone.*

He grinned as he removed his hand and pulled down her skirt, then stood. "May I have this dance, honey?"

Zack and Skylar exchanged glances that made Rylie feel like they knew what Clay had been doing to her.

"I'll honey you in a minute," she muttered, and took the hand that he offered.

Clay led her to the edge of the dance floor, where they were in shadow. Even though the band was playing a fairly fast tune, he pulled her close so that their bodies melded together. He rested his hands on her hips, just above her ass while she hooked her hands around his neck and smiled up at him.

Damn, but he was handsome. That sexy smile, the way he looked at her like he intended to eat her all up. She loved the feel of his body pressed tight to hers. She loved his masculine scent, the way it surrounded her and made her feel content, and loved.

She loved . . . him.

Oh, God.

A tingling sensation rushed through her as the realization filled her with a strange combination of exhilaration and outright terror. She knew she'd been fighting it all along—but was she ready to face those feelings now?

Clay pressed his cheek against hers, his stubble rough against her skin. "I can't wait to get you alone, honey."

"Yeah." She turned her face so that her lips were close to his. "Just kiss me already."

A rumble rose in his chest, reverberating through her as he

claimed her mouth. His lips were gentle at first, but then grew hungrier as their bodies continued to sway to the music.

Everything faded around Rylie until all she was aware of was the man in her arms, and the knowledge that the impossible had happened.

Rylie Thorn had fallen totally, completely, absolutely, in love with Clay Wayland.

When they finally left the reception, Rylie was so aroused she could hardly stand it. "Turn here." She pointed to the entrance of a dirt road that led to the mountains behind the Thorn Ranch.

"What do you have in mind?" Clay gave her a quick look as he guided the truck down the road she suggested.

In response, she lifted the hem of her blouse, yanked it over her head, and then unclasped her bra and tossed it to the floor. "You. Right here. Right now." She shimmied out of her skirt and kicked off her shoes.

Clay groaned and shifted in his seat. "I'm about ready to pull the truck over."

Rylie knelt on the seat next to him, her naked body pressed tight along his biceps. "Just keep driving till I tell you to stop, Sheriff." She rubbed her breasts against his shirt, the material chaffing her sensitive nipples.

He took one hand off the wheel and moved it between her thighs, easing it up to cup her sex. Moaning, she thrust her hips against his hand. The scent of her juices mingled with his light aftershave and the truck's leather interior.

She nuzzled his neck, drinking in the smell of him. "You should keep hold of the wheel."

Clay flicked his finger against her bare skin. "I can't keep my hands off you, honey."

"You don't have to wait any longer." She gestured to a cleared area that was a kind of overlook. "Park by those trees."

They'd driven just high enough into the mountains that they could see the glitter of lights from Douglas as well as the Mexican town of Agua Prieta that bordered it to the south.

As soon as Clay parked and killed the lights, he grabbed Rylie and pulled her onto his lap so that she was straddling him. "I can't wait to be inside you."

Rylie moaned as he took one of her nipples into his mouth, and she could hardly speak. "No. Outside. By the tailgate."

The look that came over his face was positively untamed. "Hold on." Clay yanked the door open. He was so powerful that he was able to grip Rylie snug against him with one arm while he climbed out of his truck.

She laughed and clung to him, wrapping her legs tight around his waist. Night air cooled her and caused goose bumps to sprout along her skin. The cool breeze felt erotic brushing across her bare back and ass, while her chest and thighs were pressed against Clay's shirt and jeans.

He strode to the back of the truck and carefully set her down on a clear patch of ground that was pebbly, but didn't hurt her feet.

"Leave your clothes on. Just undo your jeans." She turned her back to him and gripped the tailgate, then pressed her breasts against the cool metal. It felt so good rubbing herself across the metal as she waited for Clay to free himself from his jeans. *"Hurry."*

He chuckled. "You're something else, honey."

Rylie looked over her shoulder as he unbuckled his belt and unbuttoned his jeans, just inches away from her. He shoved his pants down around his hips, then pressed himself against her backside.

She held on to the tailgate as she widened her stance and arched her back. "Now, Clay. No playing. Right now."

Clay gently pumped his hips against her ass, rubbing himself up and down her cheeks. He eased his hands along her slender body, from her slim hips to her small breasts. "I've been dying to do this all night." He moved between her thighs and slid himself against her hot center.

"Then do it already." She couldn't think. She barely could breathe.

He placed himself at the entrance to her core and gripped her hips tight. With one quick thrust, he plunged into her tight entrance, burying himself deep within her. "Damn, but it feels good to be inside you."

Rylie moaned, enjoying the feel of him. He was so long and thick, stretching her, filling her beyond belief. Slowly, he moved himself in and out, drawing out the sensations and making her crazy.

"Faster this time, Sheriff." She moved her hips hard against his, trying to bring him deeper inside her.

Clay leaned over, covering her back with his warm body while his hips pounded against her ass. All the while, he cupped her breasts as he kissed and nipped at her neck.

It was unlikely anyone would happen upon them, but just the

thought that someone else could drive up this same road gave Rylie the feeling of doing something very naughty. And very exciting.

"You don't know how many times I thought about dragging you into Skylar's barn tonight." Clay's breathing was harsh as he spoke, his breath warm against her back. "I wanted to take you into the stall and have my way with you."

"Yes." Rylie reached between her thighs and fingered herself. "So good. You feel perfect."

Clay brought one of his hands down and put it over hers, pressing her own fingers tighter into her folds. "I like it when you touch yourself."

All the sensations were too much. The cool air on her naked body, the feel of Clay's jeans and shirt scraping her backside, the way he was thrusting deep into her depths.

Rylie vibrated, the orgasm starting at her scalp and working down her body in a hot flush. This time when she climaxed, she screamed as loud as she could and she barely heard Clay's groan as he came.

It felt like every bit of desire for this man came tearing from her lips, hurtling into the night and echoing throughout the valley spread out below.

Chapter 13

"Sorry, boss, but I think it's as bad as it looks."

Quinn had a hang-dog expression on his movie-star face as Clay stared at FBI printouts of banking activity and the contents confiscated from Levi Thorn's safety deposit box. Another ten thousand, cold cash. Deed to the Thorn Ranch. And a ledger, stored in plastic and completely print-free, as if somebody kept it with the intention of leaving no identifying evidence.

He'd opened the ledger to find Vehicle Identification Numbers numbers, dates, and cash sale prices.

Not a good way to spend a Monday afternoon.

Clay cleared his throat, wishing the numbers in the ledger would vanish, but knowing he couldn't get that lucky. "The VIN numbers match?"

"Yes, sir." Quinn sounded miserable, but also a little excited. "All the stolen trucks. And the cash deposits add up, too, to close to what he's deposited and stashed."

Damn, damn, damn. Clay felt sick deep in his gut. He didn't want this to be true. Levi had come across so honest and earnest, a good brother, and a good man. Plus, Levi had a good explanation for the night he was seen running Guerrero's men off his property.

Now this.

Pretty much irrefutable evidence.

Clay closed his eyes. Opened them. Glanced at the phone. He needed to act, and he knew it.

I should call Rylie first.

The thought was automatic. That was the man talking, though. The man who loved his woman and hated beyond words having to hurt her—but the lawman inside him knew better than to do something that stupid.

Clay couldn't call Rylie. She'd send Levi running, and then he'd have one hell of a mess, even bigger than the one he was facing.

Don't want to do this.

He stood.

"Get Blalock," he told Quinn. "Put him with Garrison. You ride with me."

Come Monday afternoon, Rylie was feeling like one of those love-sick airheads who she'd thought were such idiots to lose their hearts over a man. While she straightened up the ranch house, she'd actually been *humming*. She couldn't stop thinking about Clay. The way it felt to be wrapped tight in his arms. His smell, his taste. The way he kissed her. Made love to her.

Sunday evening, he'd brought her back to her ranch after they'd spent the entire day in his home. Touching, feeling, sharing. She'd come close to telling him that she loved him, but somehow she couldn't get the words to come out. A part of her was still afraid that what they had would vanish. That it was about as tangible as smoke, and that it would just drift away on the first good wind that swept through.

Yet she knew she could trust him completely—with her life and her heart.

Rylie smiled as she undressed and kicked off her moccasins in her bedroom closet, thinking about how exciting it had been to be with Clay while overlooking the distant city lights. She yanked on a pair of jeans, a long-sleeved T-shirt, socks, and then boots, preparing to go work in the barn with Sassafras.

On her way out, she grabbed her sheepskin-lined jacket off the coat rack by the door, slipped it on, and then headed outside. Overnight, the sky had turned dark with clouds that threatened rain, and the nippy air chilled her cheeks.

Levi was in the barn, getting his tack together to take Shadow Warrior out, probably trying to gentle him enough for the Somerville boy to ride him.

Yeah. Good luck with that.

Sassafras stuck her head over her stall door and whickered at Rylie for attention. Rylie rubbed Sass's nose while she studied Levi. "When are you going to tell me about what you've been doing with David Somerville? Not to mention Chloe."

Levi shrugged as he took a halter down off the wall and hooked it over a sawhorse by the stall. "Not much to tell. You heard it all at the reception."

"Yeah. Right." Rylie rolled her eyes. "So, the Somervilles are the reason you've been sneaking off every afternoon. And you're just too macho to admit that you're doing something nice and working with this kid, restoring and modifying the old Karchner place, and helping them out."

His blue eyes met hers, and the corner of his mouth turned up in a little smile. "He's a neat kid."

She propped both hands on her hips and grinned. "And you've got the hots for his mom."

With another smile, Levi grabbed the saddle blanket off a different sawhorse and put his hand on the door to Shadow Warrior's stall. "Yeah."

"Levi Thorn." Clay's voice came loud and clear from the door of the barn slicing through their conversation.

Rylie felt a flush of pleasure as she turned toward him, but the chill in his eyes chased away the warmth. "What's wrong?" she asked.

Clay's sheriff's star glittered copper in the dim light of the barn as he strode to where she and Levi stood. Deputy Quinn's expression was unreadable behind his mirrored sunglasses as he followed close behind Clay, and out in the drive, Rylie saw another car with Blalock and Garrison standing beside it.

"I'm real sorry I have to do this." Clay's gaze flicked from Rylie to Levi. "Levi Thorn, you're under arrest for suspicion of seventeen counts of grand theft auto."

Even as Clay spoke, Quinn held the handcuffs and eased behind Levi. Rylie's ears rang, and a ball of acid rolled in her stomach.

"Hold on." Levi dropped the horse blanket and raised his hands in front of him as though holding the men back. "What the hell are you talking about?"

"We've got a lot of evidence." Clay's face was stony, his eyes remote and focused only on Levi. "I don't have a choice about this. We've got the contents of your safety deposit box."

"Are you out of your mind?" Rylie clenched her fists at her sides. "There's no way that Levi has had anything to do with those trucks getting stolen. *Our* trucks got stolen, too, remember?"

"Where's he been every night?" Clay's green eyes were cool as they met hers. "Where do you think he got the money for that water heater? And what about a total of twenty grand in his account across the last month, and another ten in his safety deposit box?"

"Thirty grand?" Rylie repeated, unable to believe she'd heard right.

Levi shook his head. "There's only ten left. And I can explain all of it. I've got receipts."

Her gaze swung on Levi as she tried to process what he'd just said. "Thirty. Thousand. Dollars." She blinked at him. "Where the hell did you get that kind of money?"

"Like I said, I can explain the money." He turned his attention back to Clay. "There's just the ten left, from my box, right? Is that what's got you so upset?"

"You're gonna have to come on down and work it out at the county jail." Clay sighed and nodded to Quinn.

The deputy began reciting Levi's Miranda rights as he jerked Levi's arms behind his back then cuffed him. While Quinn patted Levi down, his voice droned on like so much background noise.

Rylie could only stare, barely hearing the words as the deputy told Levi he had the right to remain silent. Had the right to an attorney. How everything he said could be held against him in a court of law.

"I'm innocent," she heard Levi say to her over the roar in her ears as her eyes met his. "It's no problem. We'll get this straightened out."

"I'll—I'll call a lawyer." She raked her hand through her hair, watching Deputy Quinn escort her brother from the barn. She wanted to scream. Wanted to cry. Wanted to turn to Clay, the man she'd thought she'd loved. The man she thought had loved her.

"I'm sorry, honey." Clay's voice was low, breaking into her frenzy. "I didn't want to have to do this."

"You bastard." She cut her gaze from the barn door to Clay's face. "You used me. You screwed me just so that you could get information on Levi."

His frown deepened. "That's not true and you know it, Rylie." He sighed and started to reach for her, as if he wanted to comfort her, then dropped his hand at his side. "I've got to go now. We'll talk later."

"Like hell we will." She raised her chin, her vision practically red from her fury. "This is all the talking I'm going to do."

With everything she had, she slammed her fist into his gut.

Her blow caught him by surprise, but he only gritted his teeth as his hand shot out and caught her by the wrist. "You and I, we're not done. I'll be back tonight when I can."

"Screw you." She jerked her hand and he let it go. "And not literally. Ever again. You and I are through in every possible way. Just stay the hell away from me, *Sheriff.*"

She turned and marched out of the barn and toward the house.

Deputy Quinn was waiting beside the sheriff's department's SUV, but even with his dark glasses on she was sure he was watching her. She saw Levi through the back window of the vehicle, looking straight ahead, his jaw set.

Her knuckles throbbed as she hurried up the stairs, and she felt the heat of Clay's gaze on her back. She hoped his gut hurt as much as her hand did. Should have gone for his balls instead.

Rylie flung open the screen door and shoved open the door to the house, then slammed it behind her. After locking the door, she ripped off her jacket and slung it across the room, wishing she had something big and heavy to throw at Clay Wayland's head.

The bastard. The *bastard*!

When Rylie had calmed down enough that she could talk without screaming, she called Skylar to see if her friend could refer her to a good attorney. Skylar was as shocked as Rylie at Levi's arrest, and promised to do what she could to help him.

"We all know there's no way he had anything to do with the thefts," Skylar said after giving Rylie the number of her attorney. "Levi's a good guy."

After calling Janet Jimenez, the attorney, and arranging for the woman to go to the county jail to meet with Levi, Rylie hung up and paced the floor of her kitchen, tugging at her earlobe so hard it was a wonder she didn't tear her damn earring out. Her boot steps thunked across the linoleum as she tried to force from her mind thoughts of various methods she could use to kill a certain county sheriff, in a rather painful fashion, and still make it look like an accident.

Rylie sighed and shoved her hair out of her face with both hands. *I need to give it a rest.* Planning all the ways she could string Clay up for using her and breaking her heart wasn't real constructive right now. But it sure felt good.

Instead, she needed to concentrate on trying to figure out what to do next, and how to help Levi. Where in the world had he come up with *ten thousand dollars?* Never mind thirty. Why hadn't he told her?

She braced her hands on the kitchen sink and stared out the window. The late-afternoon sun was setting low over the mountains. Not too much longer and it would be dark.

Then it dawned on her. However Levi had gotten that cash, it had to have something to do with Chloe Somerville. That's where he'd been going every day. He'd as good as admitted it in the barn.

Energized by actually doing something toward helping her brother, Rylie snatched up her jacket from where she'd thrown it, grabbed her truck key from the hook in the kitchen, bolted out the door, and jogged down the steps.

She and Chloe Somerville were gonna have a talk.

After she climbed in and started up the old workhorse of a junk truck, she gunned the engine and headed as fast as she safely could to the old Karchner place. It had been years since Rylie had been there. Her fingers tapped an impatient rhythm against the steering wheel and her thoughts wandered while she drove the beat-up truck the two miles north.

She used to ride Sassafras over to visit Mrs. Karchner, an elderly woman who always had a plate of cookies and a good story to tell about the old days. Not to mention the woman could play a mean game of Scrabble. Rylie had never seen much of Old Man Karchner. Even though he'd been in his late seventies back then, he'd always been out working in his garden, and he never did have anything to say the times she did run across him. One of those strong, silent types, she supposed.

When Mrs. Karchner passed away, Rylie had been devastated. She still missed the old woman. Her stomach clenched as she remembered the woman's lilac perfume and the home's comforting smells of fresh-baked cookies and hot apple pie. Mrs. Karchner had been more like a mom to Rylie than any of the number of wives her father had brought through her own home. And her "real" mother . . . well, it'd been years since Rylie had seen her. She didn't even know if the woman was alive any longer.

Chloe Somerville was in the front yard when Rylie drove up. The woman had on a pair of work gloves, and she was pruning one of the weeping willow trees in the front yard, right near a brand-spanking-new landscaped wooden wheelchair ramp. Out near the barn in the backyard, Rylie saw David in his wheelchair playing with a golden retriever.

When Rylie climbed out of the truck, Chloe tossed the pruning shears onto the dead grass at her feet. She shucked off her gloves, leaving them with the garden tool before walking up to Rylie. A smile lit Chloe's face until she got a good look at Rylie's expression.

"Levi?" Chloe's hand went to her heart as if trying to calm it. "Did something happen to him? Is he all right?"

Rylie shoved her hands in her front pockets. "He's been arrested."

"What?" Shock registered on the woman's face, her palm going from her chest to her mouth. "Why?"

"That's what I'm trying to figure out." Rylie explained what Clay had said when he'd arrested Levi. "It sounds like the biggest thing they've got is a shitload of money deposited into his account right around the time the truck thefts started, and coinciding with the recent hits. They found ten grand in his safety deposit box, too."

Chloe took a deep breath and pushed her black hair off her forehead with one hand. "That ten thousand is perfectly legal. It's a lump sum grant payment." She gestured toward the barn where David was laughing and doing wheelies in his wheelchair. "A private organization provided the grant for my son to have extensive therapy to help him rehabilitate after his spinal-cord injury, and I signed a contract with your brother to work with David. I gave him the money up front because I know he'll do the hours, and I knew it would help you out at the ranch."

Rylie tilted her head. "You hired my brother?"

"He's been my son's companion for a couple of months now, taking him on horseback rides every afternoon." The woman gave a quick smile. "Levi plans to start a full-time therapeutic horseback program for kids with CP and spinal-cord injuries. He's also looking into a license for home modifications—that's where the other money came from. I paid it to him to buy supplies to remodel the house, and for his time and work."

"And every evening . . ." Rylie let her voice trail off as she studied Chloe.

A flush stole over Chloe face. "When I get David settled down for the night, Levi and I do spend time together." She gestured with one hand toward Douglas. "Sometimes my mother comes down from Bisbee to watch David while Levi and I go out."

Okay, after she did away with Clay, Rylie was going to kill her big brother. Nothing like keeping his entire life secret from his little sister. *The jerk.*

At Rylie's frown, Chloe's face fell. "You don't approve, do you," she said. A statement, not a question.

"It's not that." Rylie shook her head. "I just don't understand why he kept this all secret from me."

"Levi has a hard time opening up." Chloe sighed and gave a wry smile. "He's a hard man to get anything out of, but once we reached a certain point in our relationship, we both began sharing our dreams. It seemed to scare him a lot. I don't think he planned to be serious about anybody. Ever."

Rylie felt like she'd been kicked in the gut.

That sounded familiar.

And, she was Levi's sister, yet she'd never taken the time to find out if he had any dreams beyond trying to make the ranch productive. She sighed. "All right. So Levi has a secret life he didn't bother to tell me about. But I guess I didn't ask, either, except to badger him when I got curious. Not exactly the way to get a man— especially a stubborn big brother—to spill his secrets."

Chloe pursed her lips, and then shook her head. "I'd better go call Mom to see if she can watch David." She scooped up the gloves and pruning shears. "I've got all the grant paperwork for the ten thousand, and the contract and payment agreements, and receipts for all the money I've ever given him. I even have the plans for the riding program. I'll take it all down to the county jail. And I've got to tell them that he's been with me until late, just about every single night, even on the nights of the thefts."

Rylie quirked a brow. "Sounds like the two of you had some fun."

Chloe gave Rylie a smile. "We found whatever time and whatever place we could, to be alone."

"I understand," Rylie said, and her belly clenched at the thought of Clay. *Or, at least I did until the man I thought I loved turned out to be an opportunistic jackass.* "I've got something to check out, too. Something that might help Levi in case everything you're taking to Mr. High-and-Mighty Sheriff Wayland doesn't do the trick. Tell Levi to call me later—and if they don't let him go after they see your papers, you leave me a message."

"I'll do it." Chloe said. Then she took off into the house to call her mother.

Chapter 14

By the time Rylie arrived home, it was dark and she had every-thing worked out in her mind. She knew exactly what she needed to do and how she'd go about it.

It's not Reggie. That's just my nerves talking.

Whoever was behind this, it was local boys, for sure: maybe not Guerrero's bunch, but people who knew the lay of the land.

Rylie prepared with single-minded determination, putting on her tennis shoes rather than her boots. They'd be quieter and it would be easier to run if she had to. She slipped her pocketknife into the front pocket of her jeans. She thought about taking a gun, but she knew she couldn't shoot another human being. Safer not to take a weapon that might just be used against her. Chloe's papers and proof might be enough to help Levi, but then again, who knew if Clay Wayland and his band of brats would listen to reason? As far as she was concerned, it was up to her to clear her brother's name and prove who the real culprits were.

The men she'd overheard at the MacKenna-Hunter barbeque

were the best lead she had. If she hadn't been distracted by passion, then by fury, she might have thought to tell Clay about it. Not that it would have mattered.

They had said they were planning to meet at twenty-one hundred hours Monday night. That would be nine tonight. And it was at the same location where Levi had found their fence cut once before, near Wade Larson's water tower in his north pasture.

No wonder the son of a bitch she overheard knew Clay would be busy tonight. He'd known Levi would be arrested, likely because he'd planted the "evidence" himself.

What about Wayland?

Ah, hell. He's too busy chasing Thorn.

The bastards hadn't been talking about Clay chasing Rylie, they'd been talking about Clay following false leads on Levi. Who knew what other crap they'd been able to plant to make her brother look guilty?

The men she overhead had to be the ones stealing the trucks. She was sure of it, and somehow, she was going to prove it.

It was about eight o'clock when she snatched up the cordless, prepared to call Clay. She stopped just as she started to dial, and stared at the phone. Why should she call him? He was the asshole who'd arrested her brother. After all, considering what happened with Gary Woods last fall, Clay very well could be a part of the whole damn mess. And look at how he'd used her. Taking her to bed to get information on Levi.

Even though her mind and heart wanted to reject that thought, right now she didn't feel like she could trust anyone.

The piercing sound of her cell phone bolted through Rylie and she almost dropped it. Her heart pounded as she checked the display. Skylar's number. Thank God.

Rylie pressed the On button and brought the cell phone to her ear. "What's up?"

"I've been trying to call to see how you're holding up." Skylar paused, her voice filled with concern. "And to check on how Levi's doing."

"I'm fine. And Levi . . . How good could he be doing when he's in jail on bullshit charges?" Rylie sighed and gripped the phone tighter. "Listen. I'm going to go check something out. I think I know who has been stealing trucks."

"What? Who?" Skylar's voice rose. "You're not about to go off and do anything dangerous, are you?"

"I'm just going to take Sass out to Wade Larson's north range, near his water tower." Rylie pushed her hand away from her face as she spoke. "I can go up around back on Catwalk Trail. I'll tether Sass to the trees and then get a little closer to see what's going on."

"That's too dangerous." Skylar's tone was firm. "Call the sheriff's department."

"No way." Rylie knew that her friend was only concerned for her, but she couldn't help but feel the twist of anger in her gut. Clay. The bastard. The using son of a bitch.

"I can't go to the law," Rylie continued. "Clay just backstabbed me—and remember Gary Woods? It's the sheriff's department that I'm worried about. I'll stay out of sight and just get some information so that I have something to take to the authorities. Something that Clay can't ignore even if he wants to."

"Dammit, Rylie, it's way too dangerous," Skylar insisted. Rylie could easily picture her friend's concerned expression. "Zack's working late on a drug bust. He should be home any moment and he can go."

Rylie glanced up at the kitchen clock. "Won't be soon enough. They're meeting in about fifty minutes. I've got just enough time to saddle up Sass and get over there and find a good hiding place."

"*No.*"

"I'll call you when I get back."

"Dammit, Rylie."

"Bye." Rylie tossed the cell phone on the counter and checked the clock again. She'd better get her ass in gear and get out to Larson's north range.

Clay rubbed his hand over his stubbled cheeks as he strode into his home and slammed the door behind him. It had been one hell of a day, and it wasn't over. He had just about enough time to grab a sandwich, then head back to the station.

In his gut he knew Levi Thorn was innocent, but the setup had been good. Of course, there was the large amount of cash deposited into Thorn's account and hidden in his safety deposit box, but he had a message from one Chloe Somerville on his voice mail, stating she could prove she gave the funds to Thorn, and that she was on her way to show him receipts and documents that would clear up that misunderstanding. Clay tossed his Stetson on the back of a couch and strode toward the kitchen to fix himself a ham and cheese. He'd better make it fast if he wanted to get back to the station before Ms. Somerville arrived.

So, the money could be explained, but what about that damned ledger? No prints, stored in plastic, created like its maker planned to use it down the road to throw suspicion on somebody else. To save his own ass, maybe. Or it could be Thorn's. Thorn had been military, then law enforcement. He'd be smart enough not to leave prints on a damning piece of evidence like that.

Clay blew out his breath in a hard rush as he grabbed sandwich makings out of the fridge.

No way.

It wasn't Thorn.

Clay was going with his gut on this one. As far as he was concerned, Levi Thorn had been royally framed. Problem was, the list of people who could have pulled off getting that ledger into the safety deposit box came down to exactly one, if he assumed that none of the bank employees was involved.

Yeah, just one guy. Now Clay had to prove it. But first he needed to eat, to talk to Chloe Somerville, and see about getting Levi to play along until he could get the evidence he needed . . . and then go talk some sense into Rylie Thorn.

Just as Clay finished making his ham and cheese, the phone rang. He shoved the mayo into the fridge while grabbing his cell phone from its holster on his belt and answered it. "Wayland here."

"Sheriff, this is Skylar MacKenna-Hunter." The urgency in her voice told him something was seriously wrong.

"What's happened?"

"Nothing. Yet. It's just that Rylie's gone off and I'm afraid she's going to get herself in some trouble."

Clay's heart thudded at the thought of something happening to Rylie. "Details. Now."

Skylar explained what Rylie had said, and the trail she was using to get there. "She was in a rush. Something about getting to the water tower before nine so she could find a good spot to hide."

"The little idiot." Clay clenched his jaw. "See if you can get Zack out there. I'll head out, but I won't have any reliable local backup. Can't go into details."

"All right. Hurry, Clay."

He punched off the cell phone and re-holstered it. He scooped up his sandwich, figuring he could eat it on the way and knowing he needed the fuel to think clearly. He still had on his utility belt, firearm, and bulletproof vest. After grabbing his hat, he strode out the door.

Chapter 15

Sassafras snorted as she walked slowly along Catwalk Trail behind Wade Larson's fence line. In the darkness, the Chiricahua Mountains loomed around them like dark sentinels, and Rylie tried not to think about what Skylar had said to her, about this being too dangerous.

Reggie . . .

Stop it.

But it was too late. Rylie felt chilled to the bone even though it wasn't that cold.

She was here for Levi. She had to help her brother, because it was damned obvious Clay Wayland was happy with his stupid arrest. He wouldn't be out here looking for the real thieves.

Sass snorted again. "Shhh." Rylie patted the mare's neck. "We need to be extra quiet, girl."

The horse tossed her head like she understood. The *yeek-yeek* creak of the saddle seemed so loud Rylie was pretty sure it could be heard in the next county, never mind the *plink-thunk* of Sass's horseshoes kicking against trail rocks.

As if on cue, coyotes sang in the distance, adding eerie to creepy and lonely. Rylie shivered. She took a deep breath and caught a whiff of piñon, juniper, and horse. Familiar. Soothing. She tried to let it calm her nerves, but that was definitely a no-go. Her heart did an uncomfortable tap dance in her chest, picking up speed with each turn and jiggle on the trail.

Rylie crouched in her saddle, squinting along the top of the brush line to catch a glimpse of the water tower. The moon was a few days past full, so still pretty bright, and the clear, starry sky seemed to add a little light on top of that. She listened, holding her breath and shutting out the rush of blood in her ears.

Nothing unusual.

Nothing but trail sounds and coyotes.

With any luck she'd beaten the bastards to their meeting place.

When she was still far enough away that she could safely leave Sass, Rylie dismounted and tethered the mare to the nearest tree.

Is this where Skylar left the trail when she nearly got herself killed by cattle rustlers last year?

The thought made Rylie's guts ache with sudden fear, and she wanted to slap herself for letting her mind gibber like some whiney, scared little schoolgirl.

Nothing was going to happen. She'd listen, get what she could, then get the hell out of there.

Rylie tried to sneak down the trail, but every stick snapped like a gunshot, and the pebbles and rocks under her shoes sounded like a smaller, steadier shooting gallery. Tiptoeing was out of the question if she didn't want a sprained ankle, so she just moved slower, more carefully, gulping in fast breaths as quietly as she could.

About a hundred feet from the water tower, she found a cluster of boulders that blocked the trail off from the rangeland. They were pretty big, and she was small enough that she didn't think she'd have a problem staying out of sight. It was too dark to read her watch. It had to be getting close to nine.

Her heart pounded even harder and her mouth grew dry when she heard the tires growling up the dirt road leading to the water tower. Seconds later, the deep hum of an engine made her ears vibrate.

Headlights stabbed into her eyes, and Rylie blinked and sank lower behind the boulders. She couldn't quite believe this was actually playing out like she thought it would. Maybe the universe had decided Levi needed a break. She hoped to hell that was the case.

The roar of that engine got louder, and Rylie realized she wasn't hearing a pickup. No. Bigger. A semi, maybe, or something close to it. Sounded like it was working hard, pulling a big load. The big vehicle whipped past her hiding place like some sort of medieval dragon, gears grinding and rocks shooting away from its grinding tires like shrapnel.

As pebbles pinged off the boulders in front of Rylie, the truck rolled to a stop, air brakes hissing. The engine shut off, but the cab lights came on and the beams stayed on bright, bathing the whole area beneath the water tower in an eerie crystalline blue.

Rylie tugged at her ear and tried to slow her breathing as she squinted through a crack between the boulders.

Come on, come on. Let me see you, assholes. Faces, names. Come on . . .

Doors slammed—one, then two, and Rylie bit back a gasp. Two men. It had to be both of the guys she overhead at Skylar's reception. She leaned into the boulders. Rock scraped her shoulders, and she willed her eyes to adjust to the glare.

Definitely a semi with a black cab and some sort of indistinct circular logo on the door. It was parked less than a hundred feet from her hiding place, and it was hauling vehicles. Trucks. They looked just like new trucks, stacked on one of those trailers auto dealers used to transport vehicles for sale. They were all silver and black, freshly painted, and be damned if at least two of them didn't look like they used to be hers.

Behind all that was a second vehicle, small and boxy-looking, but she couldn't see it plainly. She hadn't heard the sound of the smaller vehicle with all the noise the semi had made.

"At least you're on time," said a man's voice from the other side of the cab.

Rylie almost jumped out of her skin at the sound. That was Voice One, familiar, but she couldn't place it. She should know it, she'd definitely heard it before, but she just couldn't put her finger on who it was.

"Yeah, yeah," said Voice Two. "Funny." Keys jingled like somebody threw them. "It's all your problem now. Happy driving."

A shadowy figure peeled out of the glare into the darkness behind the semi, and all of Rylie's instincts caught fire. She heard a scream in her head, and hoped to God she hadn't made any noise.

She *did* know Voice Two. And she'd know that scrawny build and that fake-ass swagger anywhere. Voice Two, the other man she'd heard at Skylar's reception—it *was* Reggie Parker. That bastard who'd tried to rape her when she was in high school.

How the hell had he gotten back here—and gotten into this?

Rage boiled through her, making her breath ragged, and she had to hold back a low snarl.

She could just imagine Reggie getting contacted by somebody who knew what happened back then, or somebody who found out and decided to use it to his advantage. No doubt Reggie was the same slimy, lazy jerk he'd always been, and he probably jumped at the chance for some twisted form of revenge—like stealing the Thorn trucks and helping to frame Levi for the crime.

Rylie took a deep breath, leaning her whole body against the cool bulk of the boulder. If she'd brought a gun, she probably could have shot this bastard after all. As it was, she had a pocketknife as her best defense—and two good running shoes. It was time to go. She didn't have both faces and names, but she had something. A lot more than something.

But God, how she wanted to go settle the score for what Reggie tried to do to her, and what he was trying to do to Levi. She'd love to kick him in the balls so hard he'd forever sing falsetto in the St. Jude's Boy's Choir. Too bad she couldn't get close enough to permanently damage the bastard's family jewels and not get herself killed in the process.

She took a few slow breaths, then as she heard a car door opening, she crept back toward the trail. A few yards, and she'd reach Sass and they'd head out.

Her sneakers seemed quiet enough, and with each step, the tightness in her chest eased a fraction—

Until she put her foot down on a loose rock, slipped, pitched sideways, then crashed to the ground.

Pain fired through her senses and she heard herself cry out as she kept rolling, grabbing for sticks, for limbs, for anything that might stop her fall.

Agony—

And then she hit those boulders head-first.

After he left a message for Chloe Somerville to wait for him at the jail and got on the road, Clay made the ten-mile drive to Wade Larson's ranch in about eight minutes flat. Problem was, he had to park a good quarter mile away, just to make sure he didn't alert the bastards to his presence.

By the time he found Sassafras tied to a tree, then reached the water tower, it was at least a quarter past nine, the time Rylie had apparently thought the rendezvous was supposed to be. He drew his service-issue Glock and eased through the mesquite bushes and brush, pulse hammering in his ears, until he spotted the water tower.

Where's Rylie?

Worry battled with fury as he scanned each inch of terrain for any sign of her. This was the same spot on the trail where Skylar MacKenna-Hunter had almost gotten killed last year. Bad omen. He could see a bunch of boulders straight ahead, and he made his way to a spot where he could look between the big rocks and see what was happening under the tower.

In the moonlight, he saw a large tow trailer behind a semi, and beyond that—

A goddamned beat-up Gremlin.

Sonofabitch.

If it came to shooting tonight, Clay hoped he got to be the one to take down Hazard Quinn—but what mattered right now was Rylie.

He heard voices, saw a couple of men dragging something along-side the big semi—and his gut knotted.

Not something. They were dragging Rylie.

Fuck!

Clay clenched his teeth. He had no idea if there were more men or just the two he could see. He wanted to charge out and shoot them both, but he couldn't risk getting taken by surprise. If he played this wrong, he'd lose her, and that just wasn't hap-pening.

Plan it. Pick your shot. Then take it.

He focused on his targets.

Hold on, little wildcat. I'm coming.

The idiots dropped Rylie like a sack of potatoes and started arguing right away. She didn't even hit the ground too hard, and she kept right on faking being out of it, keeping her limbs loose and still except for the hand she was inching toward her pocket. The knife might be little, but it was deadly sharp, and it was all she had.

Her head hurt like hell where she'd cracked it on the rocks, but she'd only been addled for a second or two. Long enough for them to jump on her, and for her to realize playing dead was her best chance to get out of this alive.

"Just roll her off to the side and leave her," said Voice One, and

Rylie knew now she was dealing with Deputy Hazard Quinn. "Wayland'll make this a vendetta if she goes missing."

"She saw us." That was Reggie, whining as usual, but trying to sound mean to intimidate Quinn. Once a bully, always a bully.

"She'll wake up groggy and not even believe her own memory—if the coyotes don't make a meal out of her." Quinn's words were starting to come out fast, maybe a little desperate. "Either way, I'll have the trucks over the border and you'll be on a plane to Mazatlan. Let's blow, man. This place needs to be history."

"No." Reggie again, this time with a little more menace. "She comes with me. We've got unfinished business."

Rylie's fingers closed on the pocketknife. She slipped it slowly, slowly out of her pocket, careful to barely breathe, to keep her eyes mostly closed, slitting her lids just enough to keep track of the two thieves about to come to blows beside her.

Both men had on jeans and dark T-shirts, and they looked ready to travel. Tonight was the night they were wrapping up their operation, she had no doubt. They'd have been piss in the wind by morning if she hadn't screwed it all up.

"We don't have time for this shit." Quinn's voice was definitely getting squeaky. "I think Wayland's on to me. Everybody had to know Gary Woods had help in the department . . . shit, did that bastard ever screw me good. I lost everything when I lost the income I was getting from him, but I'm an inch from getting it all back, with interest. Don't screw it up for both of us just because you've got some grudge with Rylie Thorn."

"You knew I had a grudge." Reggie was starting to sound triumphant, like he knew he had Quinn where he wanted him.

"You read the files about her supposed attempted rape back in high school. That's why you called me and offered to cut me in on this deal. You knew I'd say yes. She comes with me."

Quinn swore. "Look, by now Wayland's figured out I'm the only one who could have planted that ledger on Thorn. We've got to get moving."

They framed my brother. The knife in Rylie's hand felt cool and powerful and familiar. *Clay probably knows that, but he had to arrest Levi to give himself enough time to get the goods on this asshole.*

Maybe she wouldn't kill Clay after all—assuming she lived to see him again. Which was a pretty damned big assumption at this point. Rylie knew she should be completely terrified, but more than anything, she felt pissed.

No, not pissed.

Furious.

Her skin was so hot her temperature had to be nearing boil, and her teeth kept grinding together. Bastards. Reggie and Quinn both, stealing trucks and letting Levi take the fall.

And *unfinished business?*

Yeah, damned straight. And she'd be the one finishing it tonight.

"You always were an asshole," she mumbled, knowing Reggie would hear her.

"What?" Reggie Parker leaned down over her, so close she could smell the stink of his hot beer breath in her face. And that cologne that had brought back horrible memories before.

Where was the fear? The terror?

All gone.

Rylie almost smiled.

She knew she was in danger, but she didn't feel trapped and helpless anymore. She wasn't sixteen, and this dirtbag definitely wasn't some all-powerful god or demon who could hold her down again.

"Well, well," Reggie muttered. "You're awake after all—and still a wild little thing."

Nobody but Clay gets to call me wild. Nobody ever again.

"Dickhead," Rylie said, and she spit in Reggie's face.

He lurched back, pawing at his eyes like she'd thrown acid on him. What a pussy. It galled Rylie to remember that she'd thought he was so handsome in high school.

"Knock it off!" Quinn was saying. "I mean it, Parker. We have to go."

As Rylie sat up, her head throbbed, but she was still smiling.

"Get out of here," Reggie growled at Quinn, and then Reggie came at her. "This is for old time's sake, Rylie—and it's gonna be fun."

He leaned over to grab Rylie by her upper arms and her hand moved before she formed a full thought.

The blade of the pocketknife caught the bastard right where it counted, its sharpened blade punching through fabric and straight into flesh. She pulled hard and twisted. She powered through the cut, using every ounce of strength from her hours and days of hurting over what he'd done to her, from her years of feeling less-than because of her father, and her mother, and useless pricks like Reggie Parker.

Parker let out a howl like a coyote with its leg snapped in a bear trap. He threw himself backward and fell beside her, then rolled back and forth kicking his legs. Blood didn't just trickle, it *poured* out of Parker's groin, spurting between his fingers as he held himself like he was trying to make sure none of his pieces fell off.

"Good luck with that," Rylie muttered, feeling a flicker of something like total, jabbering insanity.

Quinn started yelling. Rylie still had hold of the knife, but as she staggered to her feet and turned toward Quinn, she saw his gun, drawn and aimed right at her face.

Okay. Here's the fear.

Icy terror flooded her in one huge, crippling rush. She shook all over, staring at that muzzle of his service pistol. She dropped the bloody knife and put both hands up like the bastard would really care that she was surrendering.

This is it. This is where I die. And I didn't even get to tell Clay I get it—and that I'm sorry.

"Bitch!" Reggie screamed, whipping back and forth on the ground and bleeding like crazy. "The bitch stabbed me! I'm cut. I'm dying!"

Quinn's hand shook. He stared at Rylie. "Didn't want to have to do this, but—"

The shot blasted through Rylie's senses, and every muscle in her body failed. She hit her knees, eyes closed, breath hitching, waiting for the agony of her face shattering into a dozen pieces.

Nothing happened except two more shots, a lot more hollering from Reggie, and Deputy Quinn falling backward, big bloody patches blooming across his T-shirt.

The night seemed to explode all around her then, with headlights and searchlights slicing in from every direction.

"Get down, Rylie," somebody bellowed. "Get down now!"

She knew that voice.

Clay.

Rylie went face-first on the ground, her arms covering her head.

Shouts erupted like fireworks, four voices. No wait, five or six. Maybe even seven.

"Secure the perimeter!"

"Thermal scanner says it's just these three and the shooter by the big rocks."

"DEA. Nobody move!"

And then some guy, sounding a little queasy, rasped, "Jesus. Man down. Call an ambulance. I think somebody cut this dude's dick off—right through his jeans."

A more familiar voice called, "Wayland, is that you behind the boulders?"

"Hunter," Clay answered. "About damned time you showed up."

"Good shooting," Zack Hunter called back. Then to his men, "He's clear. Let him through."

Rylie lifted her head out of the dirt and saw Clay coming. Her chest squeezed, and she thought her heart might actually dissolve. She got to her feet before he reached her, swayed, then felt his arms around her, felt the hard muscle of his chest against her face.

"You crazy little shit," came his low, warm rumble in her ear. "Don't you ever do anything this insane again, you hear me?"

But he never gave her a chance to respond. He kissed her face, her hair, her nose, and then her mouth. A hard, passionate, feral kiss that seared through Rylie like wildfire. She felt marked and possessed, and for once in her life, she reveled in it.

When he finally raised his head, he looked down at her with so much caring and love she couldn't think straight.

"I don't care about your issues and all that no-commitment crap. You and I are getting married. And the sooner the better, 'cause I sure need to keep a closer eye on you."

Rylie blinked as what he'd said sank in. A warm feeling spread through her, a feeling like nothing she'd ever known before. She licked her lips, and then smiled. "All right." Her voice sounded shaky, but she kept going. "But only so I can keep an eye on you, too, Sheriff."

"Damn, Rylie." Zack Hunter loomed beside them then, catching her attention. His dark hair seemed to glimmer in the moonlight, and searchlights glared against the scar than ran down one side of his face. "Did you take a sword to this guy? He might bleed to death before we can—you know—get it all sewed back together."

Rylie shrugged, still feeling hazy and now giddy on top of that. "What can I say? He pissed me off."

"Do the world a favor," Clay said through clenched teeth. "Don't get in any hurry to put Humpty Dumpty together again. He tried to rape Rylie in high school, and he would have gone after her again tonight if she hadn't defended herself."

Zack looked from Rylie to Clay, then back to Rylie. "Reggie Parker. I remember that bastard now. Sky'll be impressed, after she gets through being nine kinds of mad that you took such a huge chance with your life." He paused, then shot Clay a grin. "Friendly word of advice, Sheriff. Don't piss her off."

Clay gave the man a solemn nod.

As Zack walked away, Rylie yelled, "I want my knife back as soon as it's processed. It's special, okay?"

Zack waved a hand to let her know he'd heard her. Then more ICE agents came swooping in, and Clay was kissing her again, and Rylie didn't want to worry about anything else, ever again.

Chapter 16

I must be out of my mind, Rylie thought as Clay led her from his vehicle.

She was blindfolded, her hands tied securely behind her back with a silk scarf. He held her close, his arm draped around her shoulders as he guided her forward. *Yeah. Out of my mind in love.*

She could hardly believe that she was now Rylie Wayland. She'd thought about keeping her maiden name, like Skylar had done, but Rylie Thorn-Wayland sounded like the name of a corporate lawyer, or maybe a bad British porn star. It had been a week since they'd taken down Quinn and Parker, and Clay insisted he couldn't wait any longer. Clay had been cleared on the righteous shooting, and Parker was still in ICU—though the docs quietly assured Clay that his raping days were over for good. If he ever got out of prison, he wouldn't have the equipment to pose that kind of threat to a woman. They still hadn't found any connections to a larger criminal operation—seemed like the two idiots were in it alone, just for the money.

At the moment, Rylie couldn't care less about Reggie, or the thefts, or anything to do with Cochise County's criminal world—though she was glad her trucks had been recovered, along with most of the others that hadn't already been hauled across the border. She didn't want to think about anything but Clay.

Truth be told, commitment phobia aside, she hadn't wanted to wait any longer, either.

Clay and Rylie had been married just an hour ago at the Bisbee City Hall by the Justice of the Peace. Skylar and Zack had been in attendance, along with Levi, Chloe, and her son David. Rylie had an idea that Levi might be heading down the aisle real soon himself.

Being blindfolded heightened every one of her senses. A car passed in the distance and a small dog yapped somewhere nearby. Beneath her heels she felt asphalt then sidewalk as Clay helped her along. A gentle wind stirred her short hair against her neck, the warm air carrying the fragrance of spring with the tiniest hint of summer just around the corner.

Rylie's skin tingled with absolute awareness of the man with her, his muscled arm holding her secure. The light scent of his aftershave enveloped her, along with his own unique masculine smell. Even if she were blindfolded in a roomful of men, she'd know his elemental scent, the taste of his skin, the feel of his hard body against hers.

"I can't believe I let you do this to me." Rylie lifted her head and tried to peek beneath the blindfold, but the black scarf was too well wrapped around her eyes. "Now that we're here, why don't you tell me where we are and what we're doing?"

Clay laughed, his husky chuckle shooting a fireball straight through her belly. "Be careful. In about two more steps we're gonna head up a set of stairs."

Her feet faltered and Clay murmured, "What the hell," and then the next thing she knew his arms were around her waist and he was raising her up and throwing her over his shoulder.

"Clay!" She cried out and laughed all at once as blood rushed to her head and she felt his body move beneath her as he climbed the stairs. The necklace of linked gold hearts and diamonds slid up over her chin, probably making her look even more ridiculous. She wished her hands weren't bound so that she could pound on him or something.

Her wedding dress was an ocean-blue silky affair that only reached the top of her thighs. She'd loved how it looked on her, and by the way Clay had eyed her all morning, she knew he liked it, too.

"Let me down. Someone's gonna see up my dress." And they'd get one hell of a view, since as usual she wasn't wearing any underwear.

His boots clomped up the wooden steps as he smoothed down her silky skirt, holding his arm tight under her ass. "Quiet down, woman."

"You know you're going to pay for this, don't you?" She sank her teeth into his western dress shirt and the firm skin beneath it, giving him a playful bite.

"Hey." Clay shrugged beneath her mouth and swatted her ass. "Watch it, wildcat." He reached a landing, the hollow sound of wood beneath his boots as he started across it. "Or I'm gonna have to teach you a lesson."

"Ha." The squeak of a screen door met her ears, and a rush of warm air washed over her as he stepped onto a throw rug or flooring that must have been carpeted since his boot steps were now muffled. She caught a potpourri of smells: warm bread, cinnamon, and spices. "You can let me go now."

He shifted her in his arms, his grip tighter than ever. "Pipe down."

Before she had a chance to tell him off, a woman laughed and said, "Welcome to Navaeh's Bed-and-Breakfast, Sheriff Wayland. And that must be your bride?"

"Good to see you again." Clay swatted Rylie's butt a second time, and she gasped from the contact. "Rylie, I think you know Navaeh from the ranchers' charity bash each Christmas."

Heat rushed through Rylie from the tips of her toes to the ends of the hair that was hanging in her face. How embarrassing. Navaeh could see her butt sticking up in the air, and she was blindfolded and trussed up like a roped calf at a rodeo.

"Hi, Navaeh," Rylie muttered. "Can you knock this guy over the head with a shovel or something? I'd appreciate it."

"I'll see what I can do." Humor infused Navaeh's pleasant voice. "Here's your key, Sheriff. I reserved the best room we have to offer. Just head up those stairs, then down the hall, and it's the last door on the left."

"Thank you kindly," the big oaf replied and Rylie's head spun as he turned. His boots thumped against wood flooring again.

"You are *so* dead, Clay Wayland," Rylie muttered as he climbed another set of stairs and she bounced against his back. "Right after I ride you like a wild bronco, I'm gonna kill you."

He chuckled, the deep sound reverberating from his body and straight through her. "You'll be too worn out once I get through with you, honey."

Clay's entire body throbbed as he slid the key into the lock and opened the door to the room. The woman over his shoulder was going to get the biggest ride of her life, just like she wanted. After he shut and locked the door behind him, he strode across the hardwood floor to the curtained four-poster bed, and sat down on the mattress.

He carefully swung Rylie from his shoulder and laid her face down across his lap, her belly across his thighs, her wrists still tied securely behind her back.

His wife. Rylie was now his wife, and he couldn't be a prouder man.

"Untie me and take off this blindfold." Her voice was muffled. "I can't wait to get my hands on you."

"You'll just have to wait a little longer, honey." He adjusted her across his lap so that her ass was sticking practically straight up. "If you don't behave, I'll have to gag you, too."

"Clay—" she started, but when he pushed her skirt up over her bare butt, the threat in her voice turned into a moan.

"Damn, you have a beautiful ass." He placed his palms on the smooth cheeks and squeezed. "After that stunt you pulled last week and almost getting yourself killed, I think you need to be punished real good."

"You're not going to spank me, are you?" Rylie sounded both worried and aroused. Definitely aroused.

"I kept warning you that I'd have to if you didn't behave." Clay swatted her ass and Rylie gasped. "And you were a bad girl, honey."

"Clay." Her voice was hoarse as she wiggled her butt and squirmed on his lap, her belly rubbing against him. "How bad was I?"

"Real bad." Clay grinned, rubbing his calloused fingers over the slightly reddened flesh. He swatted her again and her moan made him ache to take her now. Hard and fast.

Instead, he slid his fingers down her crack and between her thighs to the shaved skin he so loved to touch, and she spread her legs a little, giving him better access. The scent of Rylie's juices mingled with her vanilla musk scent, and he had to taste her.

"Please . . ." she groaned as he dipped his fingers into her creamy heat.

"Damn, but you're wet." Clay moved his fingers within her folds, then thrust them into her core. "But you still need to be punished before we can get any relief."

"Clay." She gasped and pushed her hips against his hand.

He drew his fingers out of her and brought them to his mouth, tasting her juices before delving back into her wetness. When his fingers were slick again, he trailed them over her crack to her cheeks, smoothing her fluids over her. And then swatted the flat of his hand against her ass again.

Rylie cried out, damn near climaxing when he spanked her. Her ass tingled, thighs trembled, and abs tightened, her body so stimulated that one touch would send her over.

The man was about to drive her out of her mind. She never realized how much of a turn-on being tied up, blindfolded, and spanked would be. It felt unbelievably erotic lying across Clay's lap, her skirt up to her hips and her ass bared to him.

"Are you going to be a good girl now?" He rubbed his hand over the cheeks that still stung from that last swat.

"Bastard," she muttered, and then gasped as he spanked her again.

"Do you need another reminder?" His voice thrummed with arousal, his erection pressing against her belly, and she knew he was as worked up as she was. "Or are you going to apologize for misbehaving?"

"Why should I—" Her words died in her throat as he swatted her. Oh, God, she had to come. She was so damn close.

"Well?" Clay rubbed her ass cheeks, then moved his hand down to cup her sex and just held it there.

The bastard. He knew what he was doing to her.

Rylie swallowed. "I-I'm sorry."

He cupped his hand tighter, but didn't do anything more, didn't do what she needed him to. "And?"

"I promise I'll be good." Rylie squirmed on his lap. "Clay. *Please.*"

Clay slapped her ass again, the stinging sensation going straight to her core. Even as she cried out, he slipped a couple of fingers into her folds and thrust into her. "You feel good. I've got to have you."

"Yes." Rylie's thoughts whirled, her body so close to the edge. Clay flicked her aching center with his thumb, and all it took was one time to send her straight over the cliff.

She shrieked and clenched her thighs tight around his hand, her body jerking against his thighs. A dizzy sensation swirled through her, magnified by being upside down for so long.

Some part of her recognized that Clay was removing the scarf that bound her hands. Her body continued to throb from her orgasm as he massaged her wrists, and then she felt him tugging on the tie to the scarf around her eyes and freeing it before rolling her over and cradling her in his arms. Her heart necklace slid back down around her neck, feeling cool against her skin.

Rylie blinked up at the incredibly handsome man that held her tight. "I owe you, big guy," she murmured.

"Oh?" His slow sexy grin sent more tingles all through her. "Do I need to spank you again?"

She moved her hand up to his face and cupped his cheek, rubbing her palm against his stubble. "It's my turn, Sheriff."

"Uh, no." He shook his head. "I can't say that I'd let you spank me."

Rylie smiled. "That's not what I had in mind. Now let me up."

Clay slid her off his lap and helped her to stand on the bisque-colored throw rug beside the bed, her skirt settling back down over her ass. He moved behind her and rubbed her shoulders and arms, probably realizing that they ached from having her hands tied behind her back for so long. She sighed and leaned against him, enjoying the feel of his strong fingers working her muscles.

"This room is beautiful." Her gaze moved from the antique dresser and chest of drawers to the four-poster bed complete with curtains in a rich shade of cream. Long twisted silk ropes, complete with tassels, tied back the curtains.

Rylie turned in Clay's arms, slid her hands up his shirt and linked her fingers behind his neck. "I like it." With an impish grin she moved one hand up to his Stetson and pushed it off his head so that it landed on the floor with a soft thunk. "But right now, all I want to do is make love to you on that gorgeous bed."

Clay's eyes were dark and heavy-lidded with desire. "I certainly hate to keep a lady waiting."

He started to bring his lips to hers, but Rylie put her palm over his mouth. "You had your fun. Now it's my turn."

Clay raised an eyebrow, wondering what his little wildcat was up to. He wanted her so bad it was all he could do to hold himself back from throwing her on that bed and completing his fantasy.

Her palm was soft against his lips, and he brought his hand to hers, holding it tight as he stroked his tongue against the soft skin.

Rylie groaned, her eyelids fluttering. She placed her other hand against his chest and pushed. "Fair's fair, Sheriff Wayland."

He smiled and released her, but clenched his jaw as she pulled open the snaps of his Western dress shirt, then rubbed her palms up his bare chest, an intent expression on her face. She pushed the shirt away from his shoulders, eased it off his arms, and tossed it to the side.

The smile on her face was wickedly erotic as she leaned forward and licked his nipple. Clay sucked in his breath at the feel of her wet tongue flicking across the tight nub and the sprinkling of hair around it. Her hands continued to explore him, stroking his chest and abs, down to the waistband of his slacks and back up again. She moved her mouth to his other nipple, giving it the same treatment, drawing out his torture.

Clay leaned his head back and groaned as he brought his hands up to Rylie's slim hips and cupped her ass, pressing her tight to his erection.

"Not so fast, mister." She trailed lazy strokes with her tongue down his chest, pushing her butt back against his hands.

He sucked in his breath as she nipped at the skin around his belly button, then flicked her tongue inside. The sensual feeling added fuel to his hunger for her, and he clenched his hands in the soft material of her skirt.

"Ah-ah-ah." Rylie's hands moved to his belt buckle as she looked up, her chocolate eyes meeting his. "Get your paws off."

"Don't mess with me, woman," he practically growled at her. He felt raw and wild, ready to take her like an untamed beast.

"Behave." She undid his belt buckle and then unbuttoned his fly, her knuckles brushing his erection as she worked the zipper down. His cock jerked against her touch and a naughty smile curved her lips.

At her direction, Clay kicked off his boots and peeled off his socks. Rylie pushed his dress slacks down around his ankles and then whisked them aside when he stepped out of them.

Her fingers lightly skimmed over him as her teasing gaze met his. "Lie down on the bed." She ran her tongue over her lower lip. "Now, Sheriff."

He was at her mercy, and he wasn't about to argue. He eased onto the curtained four-poster bed and laid flat on his back, his hands behind his head, his erection practically standing straight up as he watched Rylie remove her own clothing.

When she was naked, she scooped up the black scarf from the hardwood floor, where he'd dropped it earlier, then climbed onto the bed and straddled him.

Clay eyed the scarf that she'd draped across his chest. "Planning to blindfold me?"

"Nah." She gave him a wicked smile. "I've got something a little different in mind. Now give me one of your arms."

He raised an eyebrow, but did as she asked. As she scooted off his chest, his mouth watered as he watched the jiggle of her small, perfect breasts, and her beautiful shaved sex. She pulled a silk cord from one bedpost by the headboard, releasing the curtain so that the bed was partially enclosed by frothy white material.

Obviously a woman who knew her knots, she quickly tied the end of the cord around his wrist, brushing his skin with the tassels. She then stretched his arm out and secured the opposite end of the rope to the bedpost.

"Uh, Rylie?" He frowned, not sure if he should give her the opportunity to tie him up again. Well, the last time he'd been handcuffed. "What's going on in that pretty little head of yours?"

She'd already moved to the opposite bedpost and was repeating the same process with his other wrist. "Shush."

Clay lightly pulled against his bonds and found that she'd done a damn good job of it. He thought she was finished, but the next thing he knew, she was releasing the curtain at the footboard and securing the silk rope around his ankle, and then to the bedpost. She removed the last rope and then the curtains completely enclosed the bed, making it seem even more intimate.

He took deep breaths, watching her ass as she bent over. The urge to claim her was almost more than he could take.

When she finished tying him completely spread-eagle, she

knelt between his thighs and smiled. "I think I like having you at my mercy, Sheriff." She wrapped her fingers around his length and rubbed her thumb over the top, then kissed the aching tip. "Mm-mmm. You taste like cream."

"I need you, Rylie." His blood was a fire licking through his body.

"After I have my way with you." She reached for the black scarf still lying across his chest, and slid the silken material down his chest to his groin.

A groan rumbled from his chest as she slowly caressed his skin, and then wrapped the scarf around his raging cock. Her gaze was focused on his, studying him as he clenched his jaw while she rubbed the silk up and down his rod. "Do you like that?"

He could hardly think straight at that point, and talking wasn't real easy. "Honey. You keep that up and you're going to find out just how much."

Rylie laughed, a husky sensual sound that caused the fire in his body to burn even hotter. She unwrapped the scarf from his cock, then moved up to straddle his hips again.

Good. She was about to put him out of his misery. "Untie me," he demanded.

"Nope." With an ornery grin she moved her lips to his and kissed him. When he tried to deepen the kiss she pulled away. "I'm not finished with you yet."

Clay was real tempted to yank against those silken ropes, but he didn't want to ruin them. If Rylie wasn't careful though, he'd say screw it and just owe Naveah a new set. He needed to get his hands on Rylie. Needed to possess her in every way possible.

She pressed her lips to his ear and gently nipped his lobe before moving to his neck, licking and nipping him in light sensual bites. Her vanilla musk scent, and the smell of her juices intoxicated him, made him feel almost uncontrollable lust.

"I love your taste." She reached his chest and licked a path down the center. "I love your smile." She eased down his body, her mouth burning a trail as she went.

Her eyes met his as she grasped his erection in her palm. And then she slid her warm, wet mouth over him.

"Damn, Rylie." Clay fought to hold back, his muscles straining against his bonds. "I can't hold off much longer."

The power she had over this man was heady and thrilling. Rylie wanted Clay so bad she could almost scream, but she was enjoying this too much. Enjoying pleasuring him, making him as crazy for her as she was for him.

She slid him from her mouth and then nuzzled the soft hair around the base. "I'll let you do what you want with me if you're real good, Sheriff."

"Untie me." His voice sounded strained, his jaw tight and his muscles bulging.

"When I'm good and ready." She cupped his sack in her hand and licked first one side, and then the other.

"I'm about to ruin some nice ropes, honey." His body jerked as she licked him from base to head. "And I don't think Naveah would appreciate it."

"Wouldn't want to do that." She rubbed her breasts along his leg as she moved down and released one ankle. "And besides, I'm ready for you."

"Hurry up, woman," Clay growled.

Rylie smiled as she eased back up his body until she was straddling him again. She leaned forward, her nipples brushing his chest as she untied first one of his wrists and then the other.

The moment he was free, Clay flipped her on her back so fast that her head spun. "Damn, what you do to me."

He lowered his head and captured her nipple in his mouth, licking and sucking it with such pressure that she thought the sensation was going to make her melt. She buried her hands in his thick hair, pressing him closer as he moved his mouth to her other breast, nipping at it like something wild and untamed.

"Now, Clay." She couldn't stand it anymore. She had to have him inside her, filling her.

"After I taste you." He scooted down and pressed her thighs apart.

Rylie arched her back, a cry tearing from her lips as he laved her from top to bottom. She clenched her hands tighter in his hair, writhing beneath his mouth. Her whole body was burning for him and she felt like she might explode like a firecracker at any moment.

Clay rose up so that he was propped above her and positioned his erection at the entrance to her core. His mouth was wet with her juices, his eyes dark and sexy. "I love you, Rylie Thorn," he said, and then plunged into her.

She gasped at the intense sensation of him filling her. Knowing that he loved her as much as she loved him magnified the pleasure of their lovemaking.

Lovemaking. Not just screwing, it was definitely making love.

His gaze remained focused on hers as he moved within her, his strokes slow and steady. For once she didn't need it hard and fast. She wanted it to last forever, to draw out this perfect moment.

Clay thrust firmly inside her. "Come with me, honey."

His words were like a visible stroke that shoved her over the edge just as his mouth claimed hers. He thrust his tongue in and out of her mouth, drawing out her climax.

A shudder tore through him as he came, throbbing inside her. His body trembled against hers, and then he rolled to his side, keeping himself snug inside her body, his mouth fastened to hers.

Her husband kissed her and then pulled back to look at her with love in those sexy green eyes. As she'd truly known all along, they were meant for each other. They would never make the same mistakes her parents had made.

Their love was forever.

"I love you, Clay Wayland." She smiled and pressed her forehead to his. "And don't you ever forget that."

For Cheyenne's Readers

Be sure to go to CheyenneMcCray.com to sign up for her private book announcement list and get free exclusive Cheyenne McCray goodies. Please feel free to e-mail her at chey@cheyennemccray .com. She would love to hear from you.

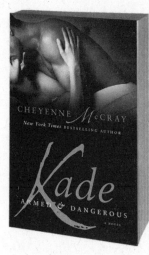
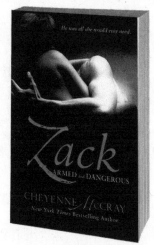
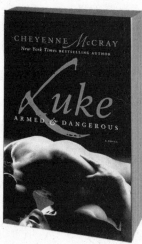